Time With Elise

A Piano Student's Time Travel Into The Life of Beethoven

CHRISTINA SCHILLING

ISBN: 1499301472
ISBN 13: 9781499301472

Dedication

I dedicate this book to my husband, Ray. At the same time, this book is going out to all of those who want to enjoy a trip from the twenty-first century back into the nineteenth century.

- Live in the present
- Connect with the past
- Look forward to the future

Love

Mom :)

Acknowledgement

My deep thanks go to the helpful staff at CreateSpace for giving this book its wings by editing and publishing it. I wanted to give special thanks to my granddaughter Taylor Schilling for her help designing the book cover image. A big thank-you also goes to my husband, Ray Schilling, for his unflagging support, his patient listening, and his help with the graphics and all the other idiosyncrasies that computers have in store for a struggling author.

Contents

Prologue

The door slammed, and Annalisa clutched a bundle of music sheets under her arm as she briskly walked down the street. The voice of her mother still echoed in her ears and made her wince. "You want to prepare for the next concert presentation at your school? I haven't heard you practice enough! This is just some dabbling with a piece that is way over your head. And what a waste of time! You have other work to do for your final exams. Think about it! Just go and ask your teacher what she thinks about you taking on a complex piece of music like this sonata..."

Tears in Annalisa's eyes mixed with small raindrops. She swiftly walked the few blocks to Mrs. Meyer's music school. She had to think that walking on the old pavement of suburban Vienna was like stepping on a piece of history. The composer whose work she was studying had probably walked along here on his way to a coffeehouse or on his way out of town in the early 1800s, and she found it fascinating how tangible history could be. In her mind she replayed a passage from Beethoven's *Moonlight* Sonata, and the slow, dreamy movement felt like a soothing harmony calming her after the words of criticism that had been showered on her. She loved music, and it was like an oasis of serenity for her.

Entering through the creaking door of the old house where her teacher's music studio was located, she quickly went up the stairs to the second floor. She rang the doorbell, and heavy steps approached. Mrs. Meyer opened the door and nodded shortly. She was a woman of few words.

Another student was just finishing his lesson and was about to collect his music sheets Annalisa's face brightened. It was her friend Mark who had been taking the lesson before her. He took a step towards her, tempted to give her a hug, but there was the teacher watching them. His eyes rested on Elise for a long moment, and she felt herself blush. Mark played the piano at a similar skill level as Annalisa. They often played pieces for four hands together. The two were inseparable, even though they were total opposites: Annalisa was serious about music and a perfectionist and planned to study music and work hard to receive a scholarship. For Mark, it was about fun. If there was a glitch in his playing, he would apologetically utter, "Oops, Mark, you goofed!" But he could not obsess over small mistakes. He played classical pieces to improve his technique, and other than that he rattled down well-known pop pieces, seemingly without much practice or effort. He sometimes mentioned that he could pay his way through university, studying physics, by hammering out pop tunes on the piano in restaurants and bars. He was already playing twice per week at a popular student hangout, as he was about to finish his first year of university.

"Just as well that I have both of you here together at the same time," said Mrs. Meyer. "You both have the one Beethoven piano sonata for four hands in the works. I know the concert is still far away, but I'd like to see how you are progressing. Are you comfortable with that?"

"Umm…I think I can do that," Mark replied with a mischievous glance at his partner. "As long as you don't murder me, Elise, if it's not absolutely spotless, perfect, and brilliant!"

"Aww, Mr. B., I'm not that bad!"

They liked to call each other by their nicknames. Mark had received his nickname, "Mr. B.," from Annalisa due to his Beethovenian appearance: he had dark, tousled hair and black eyes, and he also displayed temperamental behavior. He called her "Elise" after one of Beethoven's piano pieces. It was their private joke.

Annalisa playfully swatted him over his back with a bunch of sheet music.

"Ouch, see! I knew it! You are hitting me already!" Mark grinned at her, and they took their seats in front of the instrument. The teacher watched them. They silently communicated the start of the piece to each other, and after that the upbeat melody sounded through the room. Mark still needed practice, but they were a very good team. For a short moment their hands touched, and Annalisa cautiously glanced over to him. His quick glance told her, that it had not been simply a coincidence, and her heart seemed to beat a bit faster. But of course, she could not just tousle his hair and snuggle up to him. There was no privacy here.

Their short interaction had been enough to have Mark stumble over a chord. They exchanged a quick smile, and after the small glitch in their play Annalisa waited for him to catch up. They were such opposites: Annalisa with her light brown hair and eyes that looked clear and light blue, like a mountain creek, and Mark with a mop of dark hair that defied any effort to be tamed and almost black eyes that seemed to be forever busy watching and looking.

The teacher was pleased. "Just keep on practicing. You are on the right path. I'll have another listen in about a month's time. Till then—just carry on!"

Mark packed up his music. "Hey, Elise, want to go to the movies tonight?" He smiled at her expectantly.

Elise nodded in agreement. "You know, that would be really nice. So, see you later?"

"Yes, I'll see you soon!" He blew her a kiss and darted out of the door in his usual whirlwind fashion.

It was Elise's turn to sit down in front of the grand piano. "Still working on the *Moonlight*?" asked her teacher. "Let's see how it is coming along." Elise started the first movement, which she had prepared to play. Mrs. Meyer listened intently, with her eyes closed. She let Elise finish the entire piece. Finally she looked up and cleared her throat. "Very well done, Annalisa. It's a lot of work. Are you certain that you are willing to present this at the next concert? There are still some passages that need work in dynamics and expression."

Annalisa took a deep breath. "I just love the music. I really want to work on it. But…" She hesitated briefly. "I'm not certain that I'll get it all perfect. And my mother keeps on telling me that I'm not practicing enough and that it's more than I can do."

The teacher sighed. "You still have so much time—lots of time! You can listen to various recordings of artists, which will give you a clearer picture about the piece, its dynamics, and the emotions. Maybe we take a break from this for today, and you play the other two practice pieces you have worked on—"

The shrill ring of a telephone interrupted them. "Meyer's Piano Studio… yes, hello, Mrs. Helfing." There was an avalanche of words.

Annalisa cringed. Her mother was calling. She wondered about the reason for her mother calling her teacher.

"Well, I do not believe that it is a waste of time and effort, Mrs. Helfing. As a matter of fact, your daughter has achieved a great deal. I just listened to the piece that she prepared, and while she still has to do some more work on it, it is obvious that she has the talent and maturity to perform the piece at the concert."

Annalisa cautiously eyed her teacher. It was the longest conversation she'd ever heard from her teacher, and she was relieved Mrs. Meyer was defending her. But there was a shadow of sadness on the teacher's face.

"Yes, I realize that you are her parent, and the final decision will be up to you. I just thought that you should know my opinion." The phone went back on the receiver, and a sense of resignation was audible in the teacher's voice. "I'm sorry, Annalisa. For some reason your mother does not want you to work on this sonata any longer. I don't quite see the reasons she has, but I have to respect her opinion. Maybe it's your schoolwork that has to have priority…I don't know. Think about it. You can always go back to the piece a little later."

The eyes of the girl filled with tears. She wiped them away with her sleeve and folded her music sheets together. She felt that it was not only the end of today's lesson. It was like the end of a dream she had, a dream of playing the piece at a concert. "Good-bye, Mrs. Meyer," she said quietly and left. Out the door she went, moving down the creaky stairs. But with each step her resolve grew that she could not simply say "yes" to her mother's decision. She could see that her mother was concerned, as the final exams were coming close. Of course it was more work to practice, but her academic work had not suffered. Her marks were good. Quitting a treasured project was not something that she would do, and flunking exams was not an option either. She would go home and talk to her mother, trying to get her point across. They needed a good talk! Also, a good presentation at the concert could help her receive a bursary for her music studies. This was important, as her student job waitressing part-time in a café did not pay much money, and at home money did not grow on trees either. Her mother should see this point. She would soldier on! Absent-mindedly she walked on the sidewalk and prepared to cross the road.

Mark stood at the next street corner, waiting for her. He watched with horror as a car swiftly drove along the road. Elise did not notice the approaching vehicle. It was unreal, like a time-lapse study. "No! Elise!" he yelled at the top of his lungs. But it was too late. A flash of headlights blinded her; brakes screamed…

In the sterile, white emergency department physicians and nurses bent over the gurney and worked on the still figure that had been rushed in by ambulance. The beep of monitors pierced the silence. Voices rose and fell; swift steps went in and out of the area. Mark sat in a side room of the emergency unit. He buried his face in his hands. His best friend, Elise! It could not be! *Oh God, don't let her die*! If he could only sit with her, talk to her, will her to pull through!

A nurse came in. "You are her friend? The mother is on her way. There is hope. She is young—just eighteen years old. She is unconscious. She has lost a lot of blood, but we seem to have stabilized her. It all depends on the next few days. There is always hope!"

There were halting steps, and a nurse escorted a pale, distraught woman to the gurney. "This is not easy for you, Mrs. Helping. Go ahead and hold your daughter's hand. It's all right. Yes, talk to her…" The nurse pulled up a chair. "Here, you'd better sit down."

Mrs. Helping was crying and looked like she was about to faint. She struggled to regain some sense of composure. "Oh God, what can I do? Is there anything at all?" She stared at the network of tubes and wires that her daughter was connected to. It was frightening and confusing.

The nurse tried to comfort the woman. "We are constantly monitoring her. Miraculously she did not sustain any skull fractures, but she remains unconscious. The examining physician believes that she may have sustained a fairly severe concussion, and she may very well remain unconscious for some time. There will be more tests needed, of course. One of the best things that you can do for her is to simply be there and talk to her. The hearing in an unconscious person is still intact. She does, indeed, hear what you say. For this reason it is very important that you stay positive, even though this will be an enormous task for you."

The mother looked at her daughter. *Oh, Annalisa! Why did I tell your teacher to give up practicing your favorite music piece?* She felt devastated. Did she upset her daughter so much that she did not watch out for the car? Guilt flooded over her. She broke down in tears. Between sobs she recounted the events of the day to the nurse—her interaction with her daughter and the phone call to the music teacher.

The nurse sat down beside her and emphatically shook her head. "You must not think this way, Mrs. Helfing. We have seen so many accidents, and there are so many elements that can contribute to accidents: weather, rain, and a driver who cannot stop in time! By the way, there is a young man who seems to be a friend. He is very distressed, as he witnessed the accident. Would it be all right with you if he came in to see her as well?"

"It would probably be good if you let him come in. I know Mark well. They are going to the same music school and have been best friends for almost two years now. It will very likely help him to see that she is alive."

Mark entered the area. His face was drawn and tear streaked, but he tried to be strong.

The nurse continued. "From what I have heard, Annalisa is fond of music and loves the piano. There is one thing that comes to my mind. Bring a disc player and some of her favorite music. We can put earphones on her, and she will hear the music, even though she is not conscious. It will be calming to her, a source of familiar comfort in an unfamiliar hospital setting that otherwise could be frightening or distressing to her."

Mrs. Helfing gratefully looked at the nurse. "I'll go home and find some discs. And, of course, I'll come every day to stay with her."

Mark offered, "I have a disc player and earphones I could bring. But is it all right for me to come and visit? May I stay with her right now?"

The nurse saw the grief and distress in the face of the young man. "Yes, just stay, hold her hand, and talk to her. But be positive. It is extremely important for her. Needless to say, it is important for you too. We will only ask you to leave if there are diagnostic tests or surgical procedures." The nurse looked at the chart. "She is scheduled to have her head wound sutured shortly. As far as visits are concerned, we encourage family members and close friends to be with their loved ones anytime! And you can also call in and inquire."

They both sat at the bedside, clinging to the word "hope."

One

THE GIRL AT THE SIDE OF THE ROAD

Heiligenstadt near Vienna, spring of 1802

A horse trotted along the cobblestone street, and the wagon creaked and rumbled. Darkness was falling over the city, and there was a faint drizzle of soft rain. The tired wagonman pulled his cape around his chest to stay warmer and peered through the failing light. It had been a long day, and it did not help that it was getting dark and the drizzle was getting denser. He was worried and preoccupied. Life had been a struggle ever since his wife had passed away so suddenly. It had seemed to be just a cold, but she'd gotten worse and worse, her breathing heavy and raspy. And then she had died. It had been a drizzly evening, just like this one.

He had to keep on working and trying to be strong. His family needed him to provide for them. The neighbors were kind and helpful, but his grief was intense. There was his eldest daughter, who did what she could to look after her younger sister and her little brother, who had just learned how to walk. He also cheerfully shouted the new word he had just learned, yelling, "Papa, Papa!" at every occasion, and it warmed his father's heart. And yet there was the heartache that he did not call out "Mama!" Would his little son ever be able to call out for a mother who would love him like her own?

It was too painful to think of the future when every new day had its own burdens. At least his work was done for today. He had just stopped at a building site to unload one last load of stones and mortar. The horse trotted easier as the empty wagon rattled over the cobblestone street. Home was not far away now, but the last two miles felt like a weary stretch. The fire would be warming the humble kitchen, and his family would be waiting to sit down for supper. No matter how painful his loss was, which was also the loss his children struggled with, they were still together. They needed each other, and their pain had to heal.

He squinted into the falling darkness and was startled by a staggering figure in a loose, white dress that seemed to be walking directly toward the horse and wagon. He shouted and pulled hard at the reins to stop the horse. The animal stopped, but it was too late. He watched in horror as the person was hit by the cart and thrown to the roadside. The suddenness galvanized him into action. Despite his tiredness he jumped down from the seat and went to check on the person.

A young girl lay on the roadside. Judging from her appearance, she could be as old as or just a bit older than his eldest daughter, probably anywhere between sixteen or eighteen. Blood trickled from a wound on her head. Even in the waning light, he could see that she was very pale. She was clothed in just a loose, white gown, which barely reached her ankles. How could anybody be outside in unfitting attire like that! It simply did not make sense to him. She did not wear her hair properly either. It just hung down loosely to her shoulders.

It was all very puzzling, but regardless of the strange appearance of this girl, he had to get help for her soon, or she might not survive. Hurriedly he lifted her into the back of the wagon, and despite the rain he took off his cape to cover her. He then snapped the whip to speed up the slowly trotting horse. The closest place that came to his mind was the convent next to Saint Michael's church. The nuns had taken in sick people before and nursed them back to health. He would bring her there. It was just over a mile down the main road.

His urgent knocking at the heavy gate was answered by a muffled voice. "Who is there?"

"It's Franz, the wagonman. I have an injured girl in my wagon." The door opened, and a nun appeared. He knew her well. She was called Sister Martha, still a young woman, a kind and helpful soul. She knew about his family and had offered to pray for him when his wife had died. Whenever he dropped in while she was busy with baking, she gave him a loaf of bread to take home for his family. It was not often that people showed compassion and love. Recently he had brought a load of wood, and she had offered him a cup of hot herbal tea, as it had been a cool, windy day. He felt comfortable in her presence. Lately he had dropped by more often. Initially he had doubts, wondering whether his short visits were intrusive, but she made him feel welcome, and she seemed to enjoy their short talks.

Her face lit up as she welcomed him but turned serious at his news about the injured girl. "What happened? Do you know her, and is she from this neighborhood?"

Franz gestured to the wagon. "I was driving along the road. It was getting dark. There was this girl on the roadside. She simply walked into the road and was hit by the wagon before I could stop my horse. No, I have never seen her before. Imagine, in this weather all she is wearing is something like a loose, white gown! She looks very young, and she is as pale as this white linen gown she is wearing. There is blood on her head. She needs your help, Sister."

"Bring her in here, Franz. It was good of you to take her to our place." The nun opened a door to a small cell and shone a lantern to show him the way.

As gently as he could, he picked up the girl and placed her on the crude cot in the cell. "God bless you, Sister. There are not many like you. Each time I see you, I admire the love you show to everybody and your compassion."

The nun bowed her head. She blushed at the compliment she had just received. "We will do what we can, and may the Lord help her. Pray for her, Franz."

The wagonman prepared to leave. "Will you mind if I come by to ask how she is doing?" He was surprised that he'd just spoken his mind in such a direct way. "It's just…she seems a similar age as my own daughter Susanne." He paused and shyly added, "Only if this is proper for you. I do not want to intrude."

Sister Martha did not avert her eyes this time. She looked at him. "Franz, you are always welcome." And with a quick smile, she added, "Even if you do not bring a load of wood or a sick person."

He stepped forward, took her hands into his, and searched her face. She looked at him and saw the kind, caring eyes and the affection that was openly showing in his face. Her face betrayed her own feelings. He was such a gentle, caring person, and she had grown fond of him. Shyly, she bowed her head. His voice was barely audible, "Good-bye, Sister Martha. I'll come by in a few days." He turned and left.

Sister Martha's thoughts were in turmoil. She tried to regain her composure as she concentrated on the needs of the injured girl. She covered the stranger with a blanket and went for a bowl of water and a soft cloth to clean the girl's wounds. As she looked at the girl, she wondered where the girl had come from, walking in the street at nightfall, barely clothed. Who was she? She did not look like a young lady from this city, not like a proper young lady should look. All the same, she was hurt and needed help. With silent compassion the nun bent over her to clean away the blood from her matted hair and from her face. The nun felt for a pulse, as she had been taught, and there was a faint throb of life. Relief flooded over her. She would care for the girl like the child that she did not have. But first she had to speak to the mother superior.

Quietly she walked down the hallways and looked for Mother Antonia. She had to know about this, and she would know what could be done.

*In the small house fifteen-year-old Susanne was stoking up the fire in the wood stove. It was a cool evening, and she wanted to make the kitchen more comfortable. Soon her father would be home. He would be tired from working all day, and his clothes would be wet. She looked out into the dim light of the evening, and she felt a sense of sadness. It looked like the evening when her mother had passed away, drizzling rain and cold. There was pain, but she could not let herself go.

She had to think about her younger sister and little brother. When her father was at work, they needed her. The sense of responsibility was heavy on her. Sometimes she was afraid that she could not do it all alone. But there were neighbors. The women stopped by, and they all were kind and helpful. Still, sometimes the tears would come, no matter how brave she tried to be. She had found that it made things worse if she cried in front of her siblings, as her younger sister would be heartbroken, thinking that she had done something wrong. She did not understand that her mother would never come back. She would just wail, "I want Mama! When is Mama coming back home?"

Her little brother was different. For him, the small world around him was an endless source of entertainment. He did not miss Mama. He had been so small when tragedy struck the family. Now he was busy climbing onto the kitchen table, grabbing a spoon and hitting a bowl. "No, Pepi," warned Susanne. "Come down!" Afraid that he might fall down, she grabbed him, seated him on a mat on the floor, and gave him some wooden blocks to play with.

She looked out into the rainy evening light. The soup was ready. Where was her father? He was late today—way too late. Fear grew in her young mind. What if one day he came to harm?

She noticed that her little brother was getting tired. He sucked his thumb, and he seemed to be hungry too. She would feed him his evening meal and put him to bed. Patiently she spooned the soup into the eager, little mouth and cleaned his face. He was like a messy little bird! She had to smile. Tenderly she dressed him in his nightclothes and put him into the small bed. "Papa!" he crowed. He had heard the creaky opening of the door as Susanne's father entered.

"Yes, Papa is here now," Franz responded. He picked up his little son and gave him a kiss. "Sleepy time, Pepi!"

The family sat down to eat their evening soup. Susanne noticed that her father was busy with his own thoughts. "Did your work go well, Papa? It must have been a lot for you."

"Yes," the man replied. "It was getting late today. This was not one of my usual days." He relayed the story of the girl that had run into the road and been hit by the cart, sharing how he had picked her up and brought her to the nuns to care for her.

Susanne's eyes were wide with concern. "Do you think that she will live, or will she not survive?"

"I don't know. I feel terrible about the accident, but there was nothing at all I could have done to prevent it. I brought her to the convent near Saint Michael's. There is a nun there named Sister Martha. I am certain that she will do everything she can to nurse the girl back to health. She is the most loving, dedicated person I have ever met."

Susanne looked up. "Sister Martha! Oh, this is the woman who has sent us bread from her baking before? I think you have talked about her. She must be such a nice person."

Her father nodded. "Yes, I think you would like her. One day you should go and meet her."

"I think I'd like to do that, Papa. But there is something else. Can you find out how the girl is doing? I really hope that she gets better."

"Yes," Franz promised. "I already asked Sister Martha whether I might come by. She does not mind. I'll see how she is in a few days."

Susanne was satisfied. She cleaned up the kitchen, and the family settled down for the night. Franz was alone with his thoughts. It had been an unsettling end of the day. Pictures flashed through his mind: the young girl, pale like the white gown she wore, and the blood on her face. There was the reassuring presence of Sister Martha, who would take care of her. He also thought of Sister Martha's face and her smile when she told him that he was welcome to come by anytime. He still felt the touch of her hands in his and could visualize the expression on her face that told him how much she cared for him, even though she was too shy to speak. Exhaustion took over, and he fell asleep.

Two

At Saint Michael's

Mother Antonia sat up from her reading, listening intently. In the stillness of the evening, somebody approached her cell, and there was a cautious knock at her door. She did not expect to find Sister Martha at her door. Rarely would Sister Martha leave her cell in the evening. She was the first one in the morning to rise, getting up before the first light dawned. She was the one who stoked up the fires in the kitchen and heated the stove in the common room in winter. It was her who did the kitchen work and cleaned the hallways. In fact, she did all the work around the house, and nothing had ever caused her to be less than her quiet, equal-tempered self. It was her to whom the sisters and novices turned for help, and she was like a quiet, steady light. Mother Antonia admired her strength and selflessness and hoped that in time she would be able to take over the leadership of Saint Michael's.

Sister Martha looked distraught. Mother Antonia motioned her to enter and sit down. "Something must be troubling you, dear Sister? Tell me what it is." Sister Martha took a deep breath and relayed the happenings of the evening: the wagonman Franz bringing in an injured young girl, the peculiar appearance of this young stranger, the injuries, and her effort to look after the girl. Where did she come from? Who was she? What could they do? Mother Antonia put a steady, reassuring hand on Sister Martha's shoulder. "You have done what the Lord has asked every one of us to do: cared for the sick, helped, and comforted. There is little else we can do, except pray for her. She may wake up in time. We do not know enough to help. The only other thing I can do is send for my sister's doctor. Dr. Malfatti is a good man. He has more knowledge than we do."

She rang the small bell on the side table, and a servant entered swiftly. "Go, ride quickly to my sister, the Lady Lichnowsky. Tell her that we are in great need of help. We have a badly hurt young girl here. Go and ask if she could have the kindness to send her personal physician to see her. This is our only hope to help the young girl." The servant bowed shortly and left the room.

Mother Antonia stood up. "Dear Sister Martha, go back and rest. We will know more when the doctor has seen her. As it is, she is just a stranger. We do not even know her name."

Sister Martha left the room and went back to her cell. In the flickering light of the lantern she saw the young girl lying quiet and still on her cot. Full of apprehension, Sister Martha touched her cheek. The girl felt warm, and Sister Martha saw that a faint but steady pulse was throbbing in her neck. Thank God she was still alive! Sister Martha curled up on a rough blanket on the floor beside the stranger and sank into a bottomless sleep.

The brisk gallop of a horse's hooves outside roused Sister Martha from her deep sleep. Morning had not dawned yet, and just the faintest trace of light was visible from outside. There was an urgent knock at the door, which brought her to her feet and made her hurry. She heard someone call out, "It's Dr. Malfatti! Somebody sent for me." She drew back the heavy bolt from the door, and a tall man entered with his hat drawn over his face. His coat was wet. He carried a satchel and was followed by the servant who had shown him the way. Sister Martha took his coat and hat and hastened down the hallway to alert Mother Antonia.

They all crowded into the small room, where the young stranger was lying. The doctor shone a light on the figure and bent down to examine her. He held a mirror in front of her face and nodded. She was breathing. Next he carefully counted her pulse. What he found seemed to be to his satisfaction. He examined the head wound, put some powdery substance on it, and bandaged it up. Next he pinched the cheek of the girl, slightly first, then harder.

There was a faint moaning sound. "Ah, she has been unconscious, but she will wake up!" he exclaimed.

He took a small needle from his case and poked the girl's arm. The patient winced and groaned, and her eyes opened just a slit, revealing blue-gray eyes that looked like the clear water of a mountain creek. The doctor grabbed a bottle with strong smelling salts from his satchel and placed them under the nose of the patient. The girl stirred and muttered something. "Wake up!" ordered the doctor. "You will live. Wake up now! Do you have pain?"

The girl's eyes opened. There was a look of bewilderment on the young face. "Where am I?"

"You are at the convent next to Saint Michael's Church, with the nuns. Who are you?"

"I'm Annalisa Helfing. A car hit me...I don't know what happened after that. I was on my way home from my piano lesson."

"Where do you live?"

"In Heiligenstadt, Grinzinger Street."

The doctor shook his head. "She is confused. This street goes through the country. This is an open field; there is no house, not even a stable."

Annalisa's eyes flew open, and she sounded incredulous. "But I *do* live there, in the big block next to the store. Just call my mother."

A hushed conversation took place. "...had a bad head injury, not right in her head—poor thing. Does not seem to know where she is and where she belongs." Annalisa felt a sense of the unreal. Her head throbbed with pain, and the world around her seemed to be spinning. She knew the church building the doctor had mentioned. This was Heiligenstadt. All of this made sense. But there was no convent. The building looked old, and the clothes of the people seemed to be from another time, just like period costumes from a theater piece. "What time is it? What day?" she asked.

The doctor pulled out his pocket watch. "It is barely six in the morning. You were brought here at nightfall yesterday."

Annalisa's face was a study in disbelief.

"Girl, you can believe me; this is the fifth day of April in the year of 1802, and it is just very early in the morning. You are still feeling faint. Calm down; don't excite yourself!"

Annalisa stared at the doctor. Her voice became a hoarse whisper. "It cannot be. This just cannot be. Oh God, what will I do? Time cannot just go back two hundred years. This is not real!"

The man gently held her hand. "You will recover from this, girl. You are in capable hands. The sisters will do what they can." He turned to the women. "This is not an easy task. Her body will heal, but her mind is badly disturbed. So young…it is a horrible affliction! She seems to be a gentle soul, and she is no danger to you, yet she cannot be left on her own. But are you willing to have her in your house?" The two nuns looked at each other and looked at Annalisa. There was pity in their faces and determination. They nodded and quietly left the room.

Alone, Annalisa felt a sense of abandonment. She was in a world she did not know. Was she alive, or did it feel like this to be dead or dying? It was too much for her. With a sigh, she closed her eyes and sank back on the pillow.

She woke up when a gentle hand lifted her head and held a cup to her lips. "Drink this, child! The doctor told me that you are supposed to have this a few times each day. It should help you feel better." Sister Martha peered into her face. Annalisa looked at her cautiously. She saw the face of a young woman, a patient face with eyes that radiated kindness. The girl swallowed the liquid, which tasted of herbs, and tried to sit up. The nun patted her hand. "Don't sit up yet; wait till you are steadier. You have been without consciousness for over a day, but thank God you are awake now."

The girl wrinkled her forehead. She thought hard about a way to ask again about her whereabouts. "Tell me, please. Where am I? I am in Heiligenstadt; isn't that right?"

"Yes, of course. You may remember that you talked to the doctor."

"I do," replied Annalisa, "but this town is not the town I know. I live at Grinzinger Street with my mother, and yet he said that there are only fields and no houses. But there are lots of houses, big houses, and there is a store at the corner. And next he told me a date that does not make sense to me. He said that it was the fifth day of April 1802. I cannot be part of this time, as I live in 2002. This is not real!" She looked at Sister Martha imploringly, but the nun helplessly wrung her hands and shook her head in dismay. It pained her to see the distress in the wide-open eyes of her young patient. She left to speak to Mother Antonia and report that the girl was improving.

Mother Antonia was skeptical. "Yes, she may be getting better in some ways, but it is obvious that her mind is very disturbed."

Sister Martha wiped her eyes. She felt deep pity for the young patient yet felt helpless about the strange outburst she had just witnessed. "Mother Antonia, it is a terrible thing, but she insists that she lives where there is not a single house, not far away from here. She also claims that she is not part of this time. Imagine, she claims that it is the year 2002! She is not a person of ill will, but she must have lost her mind in the accident. We cannot bring her to the asylum for the insane, as she is not acting like she is mad. We can just give her protection and shelter. In the meantime she has to heal. She may want to be a postulant as time goes by. But these are all things we do not know." Sister Martha shook her head. It was rare that she felt so utterly helpless.

Mother Antonia spoke into the silence. "You have seen a lot as you have cared for the sick before. I agree with your judgment. It is true that she needs our protection. We do not know where she lives, and she does not seem to know either. Her reality is not our reality. There is no home she can go to, and she would just end up as a beggar on the streets or worse. Let's see how she will recover. We do not know what gifts she has. Every life is precious. She is young, and she may be able to learn simple tasks. I hope that in time she can be a helper to you. Only the future will tell us more, but we have to trust that there will be a place for her in this world she does not seem to know. Once she is better, she should sleep in the dormitory with the other sisters. Their company should be good for her, and you need your rest. During the day I entrust her into your care. You have the patience of a saint to teach her." Sister Martha smiled, nodded in agreement, and went back to her work.

It was a bright afternoon. The kitchen windows were opened to let the fresh spring breeze clear out the smoke from the kitchen stove. Annalisa had helped Sister Martha wash dishes. She still looked pale, but she seemed to like being in Sister Martha's company. With eager, bright eyes she watched what Sister Martha did. They were mundane tasks, and Sister Martha wondered what she was watching so intently. "Have you done kitchen work before?"

"Oh, yes, lots of it," asserted Annalisa. "You see, my mother works, and when I came home, I would get dinner started, or I would do the dishes or clean the floor with a—" She stopped herself short. She almost had said, "...with a vacuum cleaner." No, Sister Martha would never understand that. Annalisa realized that she had to think back two hundred years! This was like a game of Snakes and Ladders. She had been sliding down, down...and it felt just as frustrating as sliding down on a game board. She added, "I mean that this kitchen is different from what I am used to. Just show me what you want me to do."

Sister Martha accepted this statement patiently. "This is fine. I don't mind teaching you. Mother Antonia told me to do so. Here, you can put away the plates and bowls—up here in this cupboard. And it may be good for you to rest afterward. You are better, but you still look a bit pale and tired to me."

Annalisa finished her work and quietly left. She went to the common room to grab a book. Much to her surprise she found a volume with works by William Shakespeare. She brightened up.

The shadow of Mother Antonia fell on the book. "Girl, what are you doing there? This is not a book you can even understand. This is by Shakespeare, a great poet, and it is written in the English language."

Annalisa looked up. "But I have studied English in school. This is interesting! This is something more challenging than my old school books!" Mother Antonia looked puzzled, shook her head, and walked away.

Sister Martha was finishing her work when she heard footsteps at the garden gate. She stepped outside the door to look. Franz was standing at the gate, and she invited him to enter. "You have come to inquire about the young patient?"

Franz hesitated. "Yes, that is one thing. I had a lot to think about that evening, when I brought her here…" His voice trailed off. Then he continued. "How is she doing?"

Sister Martha's face showed concern. "She is a lot better. It looks like she is gradually improving, and she is a very nice, very helpful girl. She just helped me with the dishes. But—oh, Franz! There is a terrible thing that happened to her. She does not know where she is! She claims that her home is in Heiligenstadt on Grinzinger Street. Imagine, this is just open field! Nobody is living there."

Sister Martha continued. "We sent for a doctor. This was the personal physician of the sister of our mother superior. He examined her and reassured us that she would recover. He tried to reason with her and described to her where she was. He told her what time and what date it was. She refused to believe him and insisted that she was living in the year 2002." Sister Martha's voice sounded distressed. "We hope that her mind is just disturbed due to her accident. Otherwise she comes across like a lovely girl. We can care for her and give her shelter, but there is not much more we can do. We have to wait."

Franz sighed. "It is hard. Let's hope that her mind will get clear again. Thank you for telling me how she is. I told my daughter about the accident.

She will be happy to know that the girl seems to be better. I guess it affects her, because this is a young girl, somebody close to her age. She has healed from her bodily injuries, and with God's help her mind will recover too."

After saying this, he became silent. Gratefully he accepted the cup of warm herb infusion Sister Martha had placed on the bench beside him. She sat opposite of him on one of the kitchen chairs and looked at him. He took a swig of his drink, and with caution in his voice, he went on, "I came here to inquire about the young patient; this is true. But this is not the only reason why I am here."

Her eyes questioned him silently.

"Martha, I'm coming because of you. I want to spend time with you. I feel close to you. I do care for you, Martha." His hands reached across for her hands. She did not withdraw her hands, but looked at him.

"Franz, I care for you so much."

Gently he took her face into his hands. He had so much more to say, but voices outside the door startled them both. "I have to go," he said hoarsely. "Tell me that I may come back, please, Martha!"

"Yes, Franz, this means so much to me! I want you to come back, Franz." Sister Martha was astonished at her boldness. She was living here, in a convent. What was more: she was a nun. This was, for sure, against any rules. But she was a woman too. She had feelings, and her feelings for Franz had become stronger.

nnalisa opened her eyes and tried to see in the semidarkness of the dormitory. She was sleeping on the same cot, but she was now sharing the room with twenty-odd young girls and women. There were the sounds of breathing and the occasional creaking from one of the cots as a sleeper stirred.

She felt bewildered in her environment. There was no school, nothing of her normal activities. There was no music, no sounds from outside. Her life had been turned upside down, but nobody seemed to understand her confusion. Gone were her friends, her family, her friend Mark, and her mother. It was like everything familiar and dear to her had disappeared from her life now. Where did it all go? These were things that were not supposed to happen.

There was the surreal feeling that even though she had not changed, all of a sudden she had been turned into a foreign body in an environment that was not hers. There was a short burst of anger that surged in her. This was not fair! All this was not even her doing. So why was she here? Why? Of course there was no instant answer. She could not be angry with the people around her, as they had not done anything to aggravate her. They seemed to be at a loss about her and did not understand her, but nobody had mocked her or criticized her. Sister Martha had been a compassionate and patient woman, and even austere, serious Mother Antonia was well meaning.

Elise was fighting tears that were welling up in her eyes. Her life had been redirected in the most unexpected and challenging ways, and there was nothing she could do about it except cope with the changes. Was she a prisoner who had entered a life sentence, or was there any way at all to return to her familiar surroundings? All this was like in a fog of the unknown. Whatever was happening, there would have to be a purpose to her existence.

She sat up, wiped her eyes and realized that it was up to her to give her life meaning and purpose. Nobody else could do this for her. But, oh God! The changes were painful. She had to think of her throbbing head. This was pain too, different pain. At one point the pain would get less.

The clanging of the morning bell roused the sleepers. Annalisa slipped into a dark blue gown that Sister Martha had given her. All the other girls wore similar attire. Her head was covered with a white head scarf. She did not mind it too much, as it hid the bandage that still covered her head wound. Her neighbor, a young girl about the same age as her, with a round, gentle face and dark eyes, quickly glanced over. "It's time to go to morning prayers," she murmured under her breath.

Annalisa followed in the group, and they all filed into the church building. Yes, of course she knew Saint Michael's Church, but there were no lights, just a few candles that illumined the sanctuary. They knelt down, and the prayers began. The soft Latin chant was peaceful, but it did not help Annalisa to feel at ease. Latin! Of all the languages they prayed in Latin! She had learned English and some French in school, but this was so hopelessly out of date! She wondered whether they even understood half of what they were chanting! Defiantly she crossed her arms in front of her chest, but a quick glance from her neighbor reminded her to mind her manners. She tried to relax and let the prayerful chant wash over her like a calming wave. Her thoughts became slower. And she felt so tired after getting up so early…her head lowered and sank onto the bench in front of her.

A nudge from the round-faced young neighbor woke her up and brought her back to the reality that was different from anything she had ever experienced. Everybody had told her that this was the year 1802. Life had become different. Too different! She had to talk to somebody. She could not handle this. And being in a convent too! Sure, Sister Martha had nursed her and had been patient with her, and she was grateful to her. But this was not her life. She could have screamed with despair, but she swallowed hard and left the chapel with the others.

Of course they had noticed her falling asleep during prayers. Some looked at her with overt disapproval; others seemed to find her a source of amusement. Annalisa felt a sting of pain. She could not help falling asleep. She was still tired. Also she did not want to be the laughingstock of the group. It was difficult to fit into a time that she was not part of.

Three

Becoming Elise

Sister Martha motioned Annalisa to come to the kitchen where she worked. It was a bright room with a large stove in which a warm fire crackled and blazed. Water buckets stood in a corner. Shiny kettles hung from hooks in the ceiling. The windows were open, and there was the happy, carefree chirping of birds sitting on the trees in the adjacent garden. "Would you help me with some of the work, girl? So, is your name Anna or Lisa?"

"It is Annalisa, but some people have called me Elise before. That's much less complicated. Maybe that's easier for you too?" Annalisa looked closely at the surroundings where everything was so different. Her thoughts were in turmoil. She could not shed her identity like a lizard shed its skin. She also realized that she could, at this point, not simply run away into a world she did not know. She decided that it probably would be best for her to accept the fact that other people had as many difficulties accepting her as she had accepting them.

"I'll call you Elise, and I don't mind if you call me Sister Martha." It was like a pact that had been made between them.

"I can help you. Just tell me what to do. I can get some water. The buckets are almost empty. Where is the water tap?"

Sister Martha shot her a questioning glance. "There is the well out in the garden. I don't know what you mean by 'water tap.'"

Elise bit her lip. Of course! No water tap! She had been catapulted into a time two centuries back. It was better to think before asking other questions that would not make sense to Sister Martha. Quickly she picked up the buckets, filled them at the well across from the kitchen door, and placed them beside the stove. She was thirsty and took a cup to drink some water, but Sister Martha intervened.

"No, don't do that! Drinking water straight from the well can make you very sick. People have died from a bad fever after drinking water. Here, this is better!" She took some water that was boiling on the stove and steeped herbs in it.

Elise caught a whiff of mint. "Thank you, Sister Martha. I did not know that." Gratefully she sipped the peppermint tea. In the meantime Sister Martha filled a pot with water and grain in preparation for the communal breakfast. Elise stood by and watched. Porridge was not her favorite, but her stomach was growling, and at least it was something she knew from home. Food was very plain here: porridge, bread, milk, dried apple slices, and nuts for breakfast. No, it was not likely that there would be any of her favorites served any time soon. "I can do that," she offered. Sister Martha looked astonished, but she nodded and let Elise stir the porridge-like food. Elise tasted the food. "I think it needs some salt, Sister Martha."

Sister Martha looked up in astonishment. "You sure know what you are doing. Where did you learn that?"

"Oh, I have helped my mother at home. I think I told you that she lets me do the housework after I come home from school."

Sister Martha sat down on a bench and quietly observed the girl. She acted perfectly normal, and she seemed to be bright and observant. And yet…this was not how a proper young lady would behave. She was way too independent. But then she seemed to be helpful and capable.

Quietly they brought the food into the common room. Everybody sat down in silence. Elise was famished. She had just dipped the spoon into the wooden bowl in front of her when her neighbor's knee nudged her under the table. "Prayers first," the woman murmured under her breath. Elise bowed her head and waited. It seemed to be an eternity.

The morning meal was consumed in silence, and after that everybody left the common room. Elise went back to Sister Martha. The nun motioned her to sit down. "I don't want to see you getting into trouble because of your manners," she started. "Obviously you do not know how you should behave.

There are some things you should know. There is no talking during meals. During prayers, you are to pay attention. You fell asleep! I saw it. It's forgivable for now. You still look tired to me. Also, keep your eyes to yourself, and don't stare. It is good to be inquisitive, but a young lady should never be nosy or forward. Remember that!"

Elise scowled. Sister Martha seemed partly amused and partly puzzled. "Don't let anger show in your face. It does not look good on you or on anybody. Your mother is not here, so I'm afraid I will have to be the one to remind or even admonish you." After a pause she added, "But I also want you to know that you can ask me if you have any questions or if anything is troubling to you."

Elise looked up. "Thank you, Sister Martha. I will. There may be times when you will think that I am crazy, and you will not understand me. But I am *not* crazy; I am *not* insane. I am just different. If you could just accept me like that, it would help me a lot."

Sister Martha put a comforting hand on her shoulder. "Every person is different! Come, help me clean up the common rooms, Elise."

They swept the floors, and Elise wiped the wooden floors. Sister Martha seemed pleased. In one of the common rooms Elise spied what looked like an old version of her piano teacher's grand piano. Her eyes became lively, and she approached the instrument.

Sister Martha looked at her questioningly. "Have you never seen a fortepiano?"

Elise shook her head. "It is a bit like the grand piano that my teacher owns. I love playing it."

There was an incredulous glance from Sister Martha. "So you have had instructions?"

Elise nodded eagerly. "Oh, yes, for several years. Before I came here, I planned to play in a concert."

Sister Martha pulled a chair to the instrument. Music could have healing and calming powers. It would be good for the girl.

Cautiously Elise opened the instrument. She started to play. There was a sense of intense sorrow that made her choke. She was not at her home, and nobody knew where her home was. This was not her time. It was the year 1802. Nothing that was dear and familiar to her was there: her piano studies, her practices, playing the piano with Mark. But there was still music. She put her heart into it, and as she played all her distress and turmoil seemed to recede far into the background. She played a simple prelude by Bach, a quiet and reflective piece.

There were quick footsteps, but Elise did not hear them. She was entirely absorbed by the music. The door opened, and Mother Antonia entered, followed by a group of nuns. Their curiosity was obvious. "Who would have known that we had a musician here? You should go back to your work now, but if you feel like it, play something for us at recreation time."

For the first time there was a smile on Elise's face. Maybe she would find her niche in the strange world she had been thrown into. For the first time there was a small glimmer of joy and hope.

⌒

*D*ays went by in their steady rhythm, and Elise tried to sort out her feelings. It was like being catapulted into another world. One morning Sister Martha brought out a basket and handed her a pair of coarse sandals. "We are going out into the fields. The wild herbs are out. We'll have to gather some for the kitchen."

Elise nodded and slipped the sandals on her bare feet. So far she had been barefoot, but walking in the field obviously called for some shoes. She followed Sister Martha on a field trail along meadows and bushes. "Watch now," Sister Martha called. "I'll show you which herbs to gather."

Elise looked closely. She recognized young dandelions. She grimaced. Weeds! She could not believe it. Why would anybody want weeds?

Sister Martha observed the skeptical expression on the girl's face. "Let's get a good basketful of those. They make a wonderful meal. But make sure that you only pick the smallest, tenderest leaves. The big ones are bitter."

Elise nodded. She processed the information in silence. Furtively she chewed on a leaf, and much to her surprise, it actually tasted good. Of course! At the market the farmers sold dandelion greens in the spring. But her mother had never bought them. She quickly picked more and put the leaves into Sister Martha's basket. In the meadow she saw the familiar blossoms of spring primroses. She breathed deeply and inhaled the sweet fragrance then stopped picking leaves and went to the flower patch.

Sister Martha looked up. "What are you doing now?"

"Oh, look at these! They are so pretty," exclaimed Elise. "I'll pick a bunch and take them along. They would look so nice on the table."

Sister Martha let her be. She had to acknowledge that this girl had a mind of her own. She was not as pliable as the postulants in the convent who just uttered, "Yes, Sister," or, "No, Sister." In a way her different behavior was like a breath of fresh air.

As they did their work, the figure of a man appeared in the distance. He walked with wide steps, his head slightly bent, and he seemed to be in deep thought. As he approached, Elise observed that he wore clothes that appeared different than the style of clothing she knew. The black coat and trousers looked to her like a costume from the 1800's. He had a young face, framed by a mane of dark, unruly hair, which was windblown, and his dark eyes had an observant, penetrating look. She was startled. There was a distinctive similarity to Mark's face. But, of course, that was not Mark. She felt the painful realization of how much she missed him. Pushing that aside, she concentrated on the man's face. Somewhere she had seen this face before. Where had it been? No, it had not been on the street or in her town. Where? She shrugged the thoughts off. It would come to her sometime.

Sister Martha lowered her head. Elise looked up and offered a friendly, "Good morning!"

The stranger stopped. He seemed surprised that somebody greeted him. "You have beautiful flowers there. A true sign of spring."

Elise smiled. Impulsively she handed the stranger part of the large bunch she had gathered. "Here, have some; we have got enough."

The stranger lifted his hat and looked even more surprised. His previously somber expression became a shade brighter. "Why, thank you! This is so very kind of you ladies. I'll enjoy these flowers for a while!"

Sister Martha nodded. She looked uncomfortable as the stranger greeted them and walked past. Sister Martha took a deep breath. This girl did not behave like a girl was supposed to behave. Greeting a stranger and giving him flowers! What kind of forward manners were those? She had trouble keeping her composure. "Elise, this is very unfitting! Giving a stranger flowers is not done. It is simply inappropriate. You never act forward to a man, like a loose girl. You lower your eyes when a man approaches, and you only speak if he asks you a question. What in heaven's name were you thinking?"

Elise looked at Sister Martha with wide-eyed surprise. "You know, I was always told to greet people and be polite, whether they are men or women. What is wrong with that? And why is it wrong to give away some of the flowers? He seemed to like them. I think it is good to make a person happy."

Sister Martha sighed, feeling slightly exasperated. "Oh, what can I tell you? You don't seem to understand. It is not done! Don't you want to live in the convent and at one point become a nun?"

Elise looked horrified. "No, I can never do that. You have been very kind to me, helped me, given me a home to live in. Yes, I am very grateful to you for all that you have done. But I am just eighteen. I want to learn. And I love music. Maybe I can study to become a music teacher. I just cannot see myself living my life like you are doing it. This is not me!"

Sister Martha remained silent. Then she sighed. "You are young; it's true. I try to understand you, but it is not easy. You are so different from any other girl I have met."

They went back in silence. Elise helped with the chores of the day. The bell chimed for recreation time. Elise looked longingly at the piano in the room. Mother Antonia caught the glance and smiled. "You want to play? It seems to be close to your heart."

Elise sat down and played what came to her mind. She knew a lot of pieces by heart, and this helped. There were no music sheets. Time stood still for her. There was just music that offered comfort and serenity.

A voice cut through the music. "What pieces are you playing now? This is something I've never heard before. It sounds…so new, so different."

"I learned it from my piano teacher," Elise replied cautiously. She had to stop herself from saying more, as she could not possibly explain that she was playing a short piece by the composer Franz Schubert. Quickly she remembered that this was 1802. Schubert would be only five years old by now. No, it was better if she just kept quiet, or she would be called "disturbed" again. She did not feel like fighting and antagonizing people who would never understand her. She had to live in her own reality, and yet she had to live with their reality as long as she was living under the same roof. She smiled and finished playing the piece. There was murmuring in the background and applause.

Later that day Elise looked critically around the kitchen. There were things she simply could not tolerate. Two aprons were badly stained, and the rags and towels that were lying around did not look or smell clean. The worktable looked unsightly. "Sister Martha, is it all right with you if I clean up here?"

Sister Martha looked astonished. "Why?"

Elise pointed to the untidy items. "Really, I think they need to be washed. They smell bad too! This cannot be good for us. I don't mind washing them, but I need some soap." The woman brought a block of soap. Elise was about to ask for laundry soap, but she stopped herself. This item did not exist! This was a different time. She grabbed a knife and whittled flakes of soap off the block. It would have to do.

Sister Martha looked on, puzzled yet satisfied. "I have to leave you to the work; Mother Antonia is expecting me."

Elise went swiftly to get more water from the well. She grabbed a large kettle to heat up the water for washing and then poured it into a large wooden tub. *This is two hundred years back*, she reminded herself. *My God, it all takes so long and is so cumbersome!* But she went on doggedly.

When it was all done, the place definitely looked more presentable. She hung the washed clothes and aprons on a line that was strung between the large oak tree in the yard and the house. There was some warm water left. She yearned for a bath, a shower. She had washed herself, but her hair was stringy and felt uncomfortable. Quickly she decided that she would wash her hair. Ah, this felt so much better!

*M*other Antonia and Sister Martha sat opposite each other in Mother Antonia's study. "Well, Elise is certainly getting well. But what a peculiar girl," Sister Martha started.

"Tell me what you have noticed," encouraged Mother Antonia.

"Every day there is a new surprise," replied Sister Martha. "She is an independent spirit. She always speaks her mind. It is not that she is defiant—she is just jumping across all boundaries of being a proper young lady."

Mother Antonia agreed. "She is intelligent, more educated than anybody here. I saw her in the library the other day. The other ladies were reciting the rosary. She did not join them. I let her be. Instead she took a book from the shelf. It was a book by the English poet Shakespeare. I was sure that she could not read an English work and wondered about it. And you know what she told me? She said she studied English at school and liked reading it. This really surprised me. As you know, she loves music, which was another surprise, and she plays the instrument extremely well. But then she played some music that seemed beyond today's style. It is simply over my head!"

Sister Martha's voice sounded concerned as she said, "What upset me recently was her free behavior when we went to the fields to gather herbs for the kitchen. I must tell you about that. And there is another thing: I tell you; she constantly comes up with new ideas! As we speak she is cleaning up the kitchen and doing some washing. She volunteered to do it and pointed out that smelly rags and towels are not a pleasant sight or smell. She was not in any way impertinent; she just put into words what she observed. I have left her to do the work. In the short time she has been here, she has been helpful, and what is more, she is extremely self-reliant and competent."

She stopped for a moment to think back. "But let me tell you about our walk, as I took her along to the fields recently. We picked herbs for the kitchen. She was quick at work, and next she went to pick a large bunch of spring flowers, which she wanted to bring back to add a beautiful touch to the table. What shocked and upset me greatly was her behavior. A gentleman walked by, and without being asked to say anything, she said, 'Good morning.' To a man, imagine that! He admired the flowers, and she gave him part of the bunch she had picked. I could not believe it!"

Sister Martha huffed and straightened her dress before continuing. "I told her how forward and unfitting this kind of behavior was for a young lady. And yet, she had an answer to my admonishment. She replied that she had been told to always be polite to anybody, man or woman. She also found nothing wrong with sharing the flowers. And then she said that there could not be anything wrong with making a person happy. This was not said in a defiant way. It came out in a totally innocent fashion, which simply left me speechless. In fact, she seemed to be entirely surprised that I was upset.

She sighed and continued. "I asked her whether she would want to show the behavior that is expected in this house. I wondered whether she would like to be a postulant and maybe in time become a nun. She was absolutely horrified at the very idea. But, again, she was very logical in her explanation that she was too young and also that this was not a life she could imagine herself living. She expressed her desire to learn and study and maybe become a music teacher." After a brief pause she concluded her story.

"This just confirmed in my mind that we are not dealing with a person that belongs in an asylum for the insane. She does have some bizarre behavior, and she certainly has unusual thoughts. She also simply does not fit into the mold of what we expect from a young lady. But she has gifts that will enable her to live a life out in the world." Sister Martha took a deep breath.

Mother Antonia sat in silence for a moment. "Who was the man in the field?" she inquired. "Is he living here in the neighborhood?"

"I have seen him walking along the street before," replied Sister Martha. "Also, the beekeeper from Herrengasse came by recently. He brought us wax candles for our rooms and also some honey. He told me that there was a gentleman from Vienna who took up accommodation in his house. He seems to be somewhat unwell. A doctor counseled him to move out into the country. Also he goes to the bathhouse and takes the healing waters to restore his health. He seems to like walking, and the beekeeper said that he is a musician by trade. The people in Vienna are talking a lot about him. He is not from here and came from Germany, far away. A Mr. Ludwig van…ah, it is some strange family name. I don't remember."

"There is no need, Sister Martha. He is none of our concern. As far as Elise is concerned, for now she should stay, but this is not the place for her to live her life. We also should be aware that sometimes a young person changes her mind. I have seen older persons change their minds too. We are all human. It is asking a lot from you, but I commission you to be her guide. We will see in which way she will develop."

"It is not a sacrifice for me, Mother Antonia. She is a great help for me, very much to my surprise. She is always willing to lend a hand. She has never been rebellious. But she is free spirited, outspoken, and critical, and these attributes are rarely found in a young lady that has been brought up properly in a sheltered life. She is simply very unusual and has qualities that we associate more with men than with women. But maybe we have to start rethinking…Times are changing. People have new ideas. Think of what happened in France. Old values are being questioned."

As Sister Martha spoke, she thought about herself and her last encounter with Franz. She herself had acted differently than what would have been considered acceptable. Her behavior was certainly not in keeping with all the expectations of Mother Antonia. All of a sudden she felt like a hypocrite, thinking about how she had recently reprimanded Elise about her conduct when her own behavior had not been exactly perfect either.

She finished her statement, "For now we can curb her but not break her spirit."

Mother Antonia agreed with a silent nod. Then she spoke up. "You make me curious. Let us go over and see how she is doing the work you left her to do."

It was rare that Mother Antonia set foot in the kitchen. They opened the door, and they looked in surprise. Everything had been cleaned up spotlessly. The floor had been washed. The stove had been cleaned up. The kitchen curtains had been stripped, washed, and were billowing on the clothesline beside the other kitchen linens. The two women looked at Elise. Her hair was wet and was hardly anything that could be called a proper hair style.

"You have done very good work, Elise," acknowledged Mother Antonia. "But, tell me, what happened to your hair?"

"Oh, I washed that too. It felt really sticky and bad. And I don't think that I need the head scarf. The wound has healed up. It feels good." She handed the white cloth to Sister Martha. There was an uneasy silence.

"Well," commented Mother Antonia, "usually a postulant wears a white head scarf till she becomes a nun."

Elise looked incredulous. "But I am not a postulant! I never agreed. I never made a promise, and I told Sister Martha that I do not think that I'll become a nun. I simply cannot. It's not me; it's not the life that I imagined I would live. Please, don't be angry with me. I am grateful for all you have done for me, but this is something that is impossible for me. I am too young too."

Both women looked at each other and shrugged their shoulders. Elise was definitely not a girl who would say "yes" to everything that was suggested to her. She had her own will and her own way of thinking and reasoning. Her reply had been disarming and very true. She had never made a promise; she had not taken any vows.

Sister Martha sighed. "Just don't catch your death with that wet hair. And also, wear a proper hair style from now on. You seem to not have been taught how to fix your hair properly. Josepha, the new postulant, can help you." She walked with Elise to the common room, where Josepha was sitting with two other girls. She was busy doing some needlework. When she heard Sister Martha's request, she put down her work and asked Elise to sit down in a chair. Deftly she combed through Elise's hair and started to divide it into several sections. Under her quick fingers the straggly curls were tamed and put up in a bun.

Elise caught her mirrored image in one of the windowpanes. She had dreaded to wear some horrible hair style, but she had to acknowledge that Josepha had done a skillful, good job. She smiled at her and thanked her.

"I will show you how to do it till you can do it yourself," Josepha promised and went back to her needlework.

Four

JOSEPHA AND SISTER MARTHA

*E*lise walked beside Josepha. They were walking along the field path during recreation time. It was a beautiful, sunny day, and Mother Antonia had decreed that everybody should be outside for a short while. Also the feast of Pentecost was approaching, and they wanted to collect flowers to decorate the sanctuary. Winter had been long, and spring had been rainy.

Josepha looked at Elise with some curiosity. She was different from all the other girls. "Where are you from?' she asked her.

Elise was cautious with her reply. "Oh, I'm from Heiligenstadt, not far from here."

Josepha sounded satisfied with the answer. "Have you taken your vows yet?" she inquired further.

Elise vehemently shook her head. "No! I am not taking any vows. I was brought here after I was hurt."

Josepha looked surprised. "So you are not joining us?"

Elise looked at the girl and shook her head. "No, I cannot do that. I do not belong here."

Josepha seemed to think about this statement in silence. Elise looked at the girl. It was nice to talk to somebody her age. Josepha, the dark-eyed girl, had been the first one to speak to her. "So where are you from, and why are you here?"

It was a very direct question. Yet there was hesitation in Josepha's voice as she replied. "I'm from Doebling, a village not far away. My parents asked me to go here, as I'm the second in a family of seven, and they wanted me to join the convent."

"Did you want that? I mean, was this your wish too?"

The pointed question seemed to make Josepha insecure. "I do not know. I'm a postulant. In time I have to take my vows."

Elise was not satisfied with the answer. "You have to, or you want to?"

A distance separated the girls from the others of the group, so Josepha felt safe to share more with Elise, as nobody could overhear their conversation. Josepha looked at Elise. "This is the first time anybody asked me whether I wanted to be here. You asked me a direct question. It deserves the truth: I am not sure! I am not sure that I want to be here, and, yes, I have had many doubts about staying and taking vows. When I was smaller I wanted to live like my mother. I wanted to get married and have children. Or I wanted to do some work. I love sewing. My aunt is a seamstress, and she has taught me a lot of things in the past. I liked learning from her!"

"There is no reason that you have to do something that does not feel right to you," Elise replied. "You have to think about what you really want to be in life. There is nothing bad about thinking. But you have to do it yourself. Nobody else can do it for you. I want to study music. I want to be a teacher!"

Josepha was quiet. Then she looked at Elise with amazement. "You are putting things into words that I always thought about but have not been strong enough to say. And I am also afraid that Mother Antonia will severely reprimand me."

Elise was incredulous. "Reprimand you? Why? Just because you happen to have second thoughts about a decision that was made without you? How old are you anyway?"

"I'm seventeen."

"Don't be afraid, Josepha. You are old enough to know what you want. Do you want to go back home?"

Josepha's face had a sad expression. "No, I can never do that. My parents would be so distressed that I went against their will. There is my aunt though. She has come to visit. When I left, she whispered to me that I could come to her if I ever needed help." There was resolve in the young face. "Thank you for speaking your mind. You are right. I have to think on my own; I'm growing up and have to decide what I really want to do."

They walked swiftly to catch up with the group in front of them. After that they walked in silence, both busy with their own thoughts.

*lise was at her usual spot in the kitchen to help. Soup was bubbling on the flickering fire. Sister Martha prepared something that looked like dumplings to go with the soup. There was silence, which was only punctuated by the steady ticking of the pendulum clock. They had to wait for the food to be cooked and sat companionably on the rough kitchen bench. Elise had been alone with her thoughts about the talk she had with Josepha. Now she wondered about Sister Martha. What was her story?

"Sister Martha? I wanted to ask you something."

"What is it, Elise? You have been so quiet, like you have been thinking a lot." Sister Martha was an excellent observer.

"You see," started Elise, "I really want to know why you are living here and how long you have been here. I was brought here because I was hurt. But with you it was probably different?"

Sister Martha looked up. She was thinking back. "I have been here for a little over fourteen years, and I came at the wish of my parents. They wanted me to become a nun."

Elise looked at her earnestly. "So, did you want to come here? Did you agree? Were you happy?"

Sister Martha took a deep breath. "You are asking a lot! What can I say? I was young. I did not know the world. I did not really and truly want to leave home. No, I was not happy. But I agreed because of my parents' wishes." Her face had a faraway look, like she was looking back in time. Her calm and patient face changed. There was regret, sadness, but there was also an undercurrent of determination. "I was only fourteen years old, and I cried myself to sleep every night. It did not seem like anybody took notice. I could not confide in anybody, and the loneliness was hard to bear. I was told to pray harder. So I hoped for answers, but there was only silence."

Elise held her breath. She had never expected that this patient, calm woman had labored with emotional pain like this. This was probably even worse than what she was experiencing. "Sister Martha," she cautiously asked, "did you ever ask yourself questions, like whether you wanted to stay, whether you wanted this life? I'm just having some thoughts. Yes, I know you may not even understand me. I'm growing up, and I have been told that we all have freedom to choose what things interest us most, to choose what we want to study. Isn't that what you were told?"

Sister Martha stared at Elise in surprise. "You are arguing like an advocate! Who taught you that?"

Elise calmly shrugged her shoulders. "I'm just saying what I'm thinking. Is that bad?"

Sister Martha twisted her hands in her lap. She was struggling with the girl's questions and reasoning. "No, it is not, Elise. You are honest, and honesty is not always easy. I owe you the same honesty. You have thrown a few questions at me that surprised me. They were also questions that have been too painful for me to answer. I have avoided them for many years, but they have not gone away. I too have to come to terms with my life. Yes, I have been young like you, and I'm still a young woman. Yes, I had dreams…I thought I would be a mother one day. Life can be different. I'm taking care of the sisters. I'm taking care of you."

Sister Martha was silent for a moment. She remembered recent events, the visit of Franz that had provoked deep feelings in her. She realized that she had to face them. There were changes. Yes, she had dreams, had hopes. Denying this would be telling a lie to herself, and she realized that she was no longer prepared to deceive herself.

Elise looked at Sister Martha, and with astounding clarity Sister Martha's thoughts were put into words. "Life can change too," Elise challenged. "You are not owned by anybody. You can still have dreams, and I believe that dreams can become reality, if we are only willing to follow them."

Sister Martha's face softened. "What a deep thinker you are! You are supposed to learn from me. But I believe that now you are teaching me." She looked up and smiled at Elise. "It's better to postpone our dreams—for now I mean. It's time to serve supper to everybody." They rose and went on with their evening work.

Sister Martha lay on her cot, but sleep did not come easy. Her mind was in turmoil. Elise's innocent but profound questions had left her with a sense of unease. She tossed and turned restlessly. Pictures of the past flashed by in her mind: her parents' home, there was the moment when her gentle, loving grandmother had given her a new dress for her fourteenth birthday. She had laughed with delight and turned in front of the big mirror at her grandmother's house and dreamed that she would wear the dress to a dance in the village. But this was not to be. A few months later, she was told that she would be going away from home. Her grandmother had embraced her one last time. "Why do they have to send you away?" she had cried. "It is breaking my heart!"

Sister Martha never saw her grandmother again. Her parents told her, on one of their rare visits, that she had passed away. Sister Martha had resigned herself to her life here. All the dedication that she had dreamed of giving to a family of her own one day, she gave to the people around her. She had willed herself to believe that this would be enough. It would have to be enough. The sisters were companions, but she became keenly aware that they were not her family.

Pain washed over Sister Martha, and it felt like the old wounds that she thought had healed opened up again. Elise had reminded her that life could change. She had reminded her about her freedom to choose, about dreams that could become reality. It was too much. There was the realization that she had tried to suppress the fact that she still had dreams. But she could not think any more today. The barrage of feelings that had been unleashed was overwhelming her. She buried her face in the pillow as great sobs shook her body. She cried for all the years of her youth that had passed, for the dances she had never been allowed to go to, the loving grandmother she did not say her final good-bye to, the love of a man that she had not experienced, the family that she did not have. Elise's questions had triggered an avalanche of emotions and questions that needed to be answered, and she realized that it was time to face them. She grew calmer. Franz's face appeared in front of her inner eyes; she recalled what he had said about wanting to spend time with her and feeling close to her. There could be changes, if she only embraced them without fear. She lay in the stillness of the night and knew that every day was a new gift and a day of second chances. These thoughts gave her comfort and hope, and finally she fell into a fitful sleep.

here was a sense of unease. Mother Antonia had called Elise into her study and reprimanded her. "You have been told several times that you are to pay attention at prayer time. I saw you fall asleep at morning prayers, not only today but yesterday too. How can you let this happen?"

"I did not sleep well, Mother Antonia, and I'm sorry. I also have a stomachache because of my monthlies."

Mother Antonia let out a gasp of dismay. "Child, child, how can you even mention this! Don't ever speak about the female condition again. This is simply not done! Where is your upbringing? I declare I am shocked!"

Elise cringed. It was becoming increasingly difficult for her to live in this time where everything seemed to be improper or unfitting for a girl. "Again I am very sorry, Mother Antonia. I did not want to offend you." She was dismissed from the room and fled to seek refuge with Sister Martha. Sister Martha had been quieter lately, and Elise wondered whether she had been giving Sister Martha reasons to be more reserved with her. But the woman gently smiled at her when she came into the kitchen and gave her some work to do. The rumbling of a cart at the back of the yard made both of them look up. "We are getting a load of wood for the stoves again," explained Sister Martha.

For some reason her face brightened up as she went and opened the door. A man approached and greeted both of them. He had a calm, open face, and the most striking feature was his dark-blue, gentle eyes. "I'll unload the wood, Sister Martha! You have enough work to do. I see you have a helper today?"

"Yes, Franz. Do you remember the stranger you brought to our door? You told me that you wanted to hear how she was doing. Now you can talk to her. This is Elise. She has recovered from her injury—thank God!"

Franz looked at Elise and looked at Sister Martha intently. "Yes, thank God indeed! But it is also thanks to you, Sister Martha, that she is healthy again. You are the soul of this place!"

Elise noticed that Sister Martha looked flustered. There was a smile on her face, and she blushed deeply. "Elise can help you with the wood," she said. The girl went outside and helped to stack the wood under the roof overhang.

Franz looked at her approvingly. "You are a good worker. But you have a wonderful teacher too. I wish I had somebody like Sister Martha in my family."

Elise eyed the man closely. His frank remarks sounded sincere, but they were surprising to her. Her curiosity took over. "Oh surely you must have somebody in your family who is like Sister Martha!"

His face turned somber. "Not anymore, girl. My wife passed away last year. My daughter is holding the family together. She is a young girl like you, probably even a bit younger."

Elise bowed her head. "I'm so sorry. That is so sad!"

Silently they finished stacking the wood. Sister Martha opened the door for them. She offered Franz a cup of tea. "Thank you, Sister Martha." His hand seized the cup, and for a moment it rested on Sister Martha's hand. Elise observed how their eyes locked in one long, intense look. She turned away quickly. There were tenderly murmured words, and Elise felt like an intruder in their moment of togetherness. At the same time she felt happy for Sister Martha. She deserved it.

Sister Martha remained silent throughout the morning. She seemed to be preoccupied. At one point she left the kitchen, and Elise saw her sitting on the bench by the kitchen door, first seemingly looking far into the distance and next burying her face in her hands. Elise tiptoed outside. She waited, reluctant to disturb her. Finally Sister Martha looked up.

"Are you all right, Sister Martha?" Elise asked.

Sister Martha hesitated. "I should not trouble your young mind with my troubles."

Elise shook her head. "I think I know. It's about the talk we had a few days ago, when I asked about your life, isn't it? I did not want to upset you."

A quick smile brightened Sister Martha's serious expression. "You are not upsetting me, Elise. It is just so very peculiar that I'm the one who was told to teach you, when it is you who is starting to teach me about life. Thanks to you I have to think about my life. I'm also accepting that life throws changes at me, and I have to deal with them."

Elise nodded. "I know…"

"You know…what?" questioned Sister Martha.

Elise looked back at her. "I know that you will have to make decisions about your future and about being happy with your life." She stopped and then cautiously continued, "It's about Franz."

Sister Martha took a deep breath. Astonishment and embarrassment were written in her face. "Elise, what do you know?"

"Franz talked to me when we were stacking up the firewood. He would love to have somebody like you in his family. He told me that his wife died last year. And…" she hesitated. "Please don't get angry at me if I say something more…I saw how he looked at you and how you looked at him when you gave him the tea."

"Oh, Elise! But I'm a nun!"

Elise shrugged her shoulders. "Yes, you went along with your parents' wishes and became one. You were very young, and you did not even know what your own wishes were then. That was about fourteen years ago. You also did not have your own ideas at that point in time. But what about your own wishes now? And what about living a life that can change? Also, you are still living your life for others. There is a family that needs a mother—somebody as loving and caring as you! You would make a great mom."

Sister Martha looked amazed. "I have never heard anybody reason like you! You seem to see things that I did not dare to look at." There was determination in her voice. "But I can, and I will now. I owe it to myself. We can talk, and I'm glad about that. Just sometimes I worry that your frankness will get you into trouble with Mother Antonia."

Elise seemed unperturbed. "Yes, I know that she does not agree with my opinions. I just got a lecture about what is proper and what is not proper to say. So I won't tell her much about my thoughts. I have my own; she can have hers, and that should be just fine for now."

Five

VISITORS AND THEIR CONSEQUENCES

There was a knock at the door in the afternoon. Sister Martha opened the door. The visitor was a woman. She came unaccompanied and looked well dressed and self-assured. Sister Martha remembered that she had visited before. Her niece Josepha was a postulant, who seemed to be very close to her aunt. Curiously enough the parents had not visited the girl. "You want to visit with Josepha I take it?"

"Yes, I would love to see her again," replied the woman. "She is very dear to me. I hope that this is not disturbing her duties?"

Sister Martha dispelled her concern. "You'll have a few hours with her, and I am sure that she'll be happy to see you too." They went to the common room where Josepha was sewing with some other girls. "Josepha," called Sister Martha, "your aunt has arrived! Come and spend some time with her."

Happily Josepha went with her aunt, and they walked outside in the garden. "How are you doing, my dear?" asked her aunt. "I hope that you are happy at your residence."

Josepha's answer came after some hesitation. "Oh, Aunt Theresa, this will be difficult for me to answer, and it may cause you distress. Can I speak my mind?"

Theresa looked at her niece with surprise. She had always been such a quiet, almost too-pliable young girl, and speaking her mind had never been a thing that would fit with her quiet, almost submissive personality. "Of course you can," encouraged Theresa. "And what is on your mind that would distress me?"

Josepha began, "You asked me whether I was happy here. I want to be truthful with you. No, I'm not happy. I do not feel that I want to stay. This is not the place where I belong. I think of the time I have spent with you, when you taught me to sew and to embroider. I loved learning from you, and I loved working with beautiful materials and wonderful colors. My parents told me that they wanted me to embrace this kind of life here. I tried to please them, to be obedient. But I was still a child, and now I am growing up, and I realize that this is not the life I can lead."

"You must have done some serious thinking," remarked Theresa. "You have always been the quietest in the family. You never asked questions and always agreed. This change in you is a surprise to me; mind you, I believe that it is a wonderful surprise. I am happy to see you come out of your shell. This is not distressing to me at all."

Josepha seemed relieved and went on. "It helps that there is a girl here who is a bit older than I am. Her name is Elise. She was sick and came here under the care of Sister Martha. She is well again, and we talk about all sorts of things. She is different. She seems to always think about life, makes plans for her future, and does not stay silent. Everybody else here just listens and never has anything to say. She is unafraid to just speak her mind. So she asked me one day whether I was happy here. I had never thought about that, but she made me think about it."

Theresa looked at her. There was understanding in her eyes. "Have you told your doubts to the mother superior?"

Josepha shook her head. "No, I haven't yet. I'm waiting for the right opportunity."

"So you are questioning whether you should be making any vows to become a novice?"

Josepha answered, "Yes, I am not at all certain that I should do that. You see, when I looked back, I realized I always wanted to do work, like the seamstress skills you have taught me. I want to learn more! In time I may get married and have a family, and I still could do sewing and embroidery. A few years back what I should do was the decision of my parents. I never had a chance then to make my own decision. And I probably would not even have been able to do it. I will have to leave here eventually, but I will have no home. It won't be possible to go back to my parents' home, as they will perceive my behavior as an insult and a disgrace."

Theresa took Josepha's hand. "You are my niece and as dear to me as my own daughters. You can trust me that you will always have a home with me. You have to decide when it is time for you to leave. Even if there is a sudden decision or you are told to leave, it is not something you should fear. You know where I live, and two miles is not far away from here. You can knock at my door day or night."

There was relief in Josepha's voice as she replied. "I cannot tell you how thankful I am to you, Aunt Theresa. I hope I can make it up to you in time."

Theresa hugged her niece. "Don't think this way! I am looking forward to seeing you again—hopefully in my house next time."

Their visiting time was over. Usually the good-byes hurt, but this time Josepha sensed that they would see each other again soon, and this thought comforted her.

Elise sat next to Josepha as Josepha mended a tear in Elise's dress. "You look happy," Elise observed. "It must be nice to get a visitor."

"Yes, I love my aunt Theresa," agreed Josepha. "She is closer to me than my mother. I don't want to sound mean, but it simply is the truth. My mother is so busy with my younger sisters and brothers. There is not enough time for her to sit down, let alone teach me to sew, and we did not have much time to talk. She was always working so hard. It's not her fault that there is not enough time in a day. She also never had time for herself." Elise agreed.

Josepha lowered her voice. "There is something I have to tell you. You are my closest friend who I can trust. I talked to my aunt about leaving the convent."

Elise looked up. There was a small shadow of sadness in her face, but it quickly disappeared. "Oh, really? Well, I'm not entirely surprised after what you told me earlier. I will miss you, of course, but then I don't expect to be here forever. Yes, it's good! I'm happy for you."

"I'm not sure when," Josepha went on. "But it may be soon. Mother Antonia has asked me to take my vows as a novice, and I have been thinking a lot. No, I cannot do it!"

A voice cut into their quiet conversation. "What is going on? You cannot do what, Josepha?" Mother Antonia came closer to them, and she looked at the girls with raised eyebrows.

Josepha found her voice. "Oh, I am just telling Elise that this is the last time I can mend her dress. It is simply getting too threadbare. Look here." She pointed out the faded, damaged fabric. "I won't be able to do it anymore."

Elise was baffled. What a glib excuse! She would have never believed that Josepha could come up with a quick, credible answer to an unexpected question like that—quiet, pliable, submissive Josepha, who never had a word to say for herself. Well, had she ever changed in the time since Elise had met her! She bit on her lips to stop herself from bursting out into laughter.

Josepha finished her work. "We better stop talking for now," she whispered under her breath, and Elise went back to her own work.

Speculatively Mother Antonia looked at the two girls. They had been talking to each other frequently, and they were entirely opposite in their behavior. There was Elise, quick, observant, critical, and outspoken. And there was Josepha, a placid, malleable individual who had always been very quiet. Mother Antonia did not trust Elise. Her influence could be negative on Josepha. And Elise's behavior was at times so improper that it made her cringe. Elise would never be one of them. She had stated so herself, even had adamantly refused to become a postulant.

Sister Martha seemed to be a good teacher, and yet…she was not certain. This girl was a free spirit, and Sister Martha did not seem to be in a position to remedy this. She also seemed to be fond of the girl, who spent a lot of time with her. To Mother Antonia's consternation Sister Martha had also expressed that she could curb her but not break her spirit. That meant that Sister Martha did not find anything negative about the free-spirited, critical, and questioning behavior of this girl.

It was like a new wind was blowing into Mother Antonia's world. It made her uneasy, and she did not like it. It was unsettling and disturbing. It could disturb the peace of Josepha's spirit. It could be contagious. She had to think of events in the recent past that had taken place in France: disturbance, a cry for change, revolution. Was it the spirit of this time? She was determined not to allow a revolutionary spirit to creep into the strictly ordered life here. The sooner Josepha took her vows the better.

warm evening light cast its glow into the garden where Sister Martha and Elise were watering the garden beds. Out of the corner of her eye, Elise caught the figure of a young girl that could be close to her in age standing at the gate. She looked up and into some alert dark-blue eyes that observed her as well as Sister Martha. Sister Martha stepped closer. "Is there anybody here you are looking for?" She looked into eyes that looked so much like Franz's eyes. He had always talked about his eldest daughter, Susanne.

The girl eagerly nodded. "Yes, I came to look for Sister Martha. She will not know me."

Sister Martha surprised her. "You must be Susanne! You look so much like your father. How nice of you to come by! I am Sister Martha. What brings you here, Susanne? Do you or your family need any help?"

The girl hesitated. "No, everything is going as well as it can. I came here because my father has been telling me so much about you. Also, you have sent us bread, and I wanted to say thank you."

She looked at Elise, and Sister Martha introduced her to the girl. They talked about how Elise had been brought to the convent, and Susanne's voice became lively. "Yes, my father told me about your accident. I am so glad that you are well again! He also told me that without Sister Martha's care, this might not have been possible. I'm happy to see you too."

Sister Martha had stopped her garden work and sat on the bench by the house. The girls sat down with her. There was silence, and Elise sensed that Susanne needed to speak with Sister Martha alone. "I don't want to offend you, Susanne, but I think that you came to visit Sister Martha?"

Susanne's face showed surprise. "I don't have anything against you. But it's almost like you can read thoughts! Yes, I'd like to talk to Sister Martha for a bit. But it would be nice to talk to you too in a little while."

"That sounds good to me," replied Elise. "I'll do some more work here in the garden. Why don't you visit with me later, after you spend some time with Sister Martha; honestly, I don't mind!" Elise could follow Susanne's reasoning. She probably wanted to see what Sister Martha was like. Franz must have spoken to her. Of course she should get to know to Sister Martha! Franz loved and admired Sister Martha, and she could very well become Susanne's stepmother.

Sister Martha asked Susanne about the daily life of her family. The girl told Sister Martha about her days, sharing about her younger sister that did not understand that their mother was dead and the antics of her baby brother that were a source of joy to all of them. She told Sister Martha about her father and his steady, loving help, despite his long hours of work, and how he never lost his calm equanimity, even if it had been a hard day.

It was obvious that Susanne was very devoted to her father and very fond of her siblings. Sister Martha listened calmly. It was a look into how the family had held together during all the adversity that had come upon them. "You have a wonderful family, Susanne," Sister Martha remarked. "I can only imagine how painful it is for you to miss your mother and how hard it must be for you to do everything to help. You have a great deal of courage for a young girl like you. It is a difficult time for all of you. Wounds like that take long to heal."

Susanne looked up. "There is one thing that I want you to know. I believe that you are the person who has helped my father heal and have hope. He talks about you often. He told me that I should see you, because he was certain that I would like you too."

Sister Martha looked at her. There was quiet happiness in her eyes and a spark of amusement. "And so you came here to take a closer look at me?"

Susanne continued, "Yes, of course. And I hope that you are not insulted by what I say. I know that I'm just a young girl. I am not an adult, but I listen and watch how adults think. My father admires you and loves you—of course he has not told me that! He is quiet, but his face is like an open book. I'm not dumb. I've watched his face, and I have listened to him talk. If you find it in your heart, I would love to call you 'mother' one day. And this is why I came to see you."

Sister Martha was taken aback. "Dear Susanne, I feel lucky to have finally met you. I admire your courage and your dedication to your father and your family. I can't believe that you came on your own. But it is evening, and it is getting later! Surely your father will miss you at home. Goodness, what would he say if he heard what you just told me?"

The girl looked straight at Sister Martha. "He knows that I am here. He came with me. A neighbor woman is watching over the children while we go for a walk. I told him that I wanted to talk to you, and he agreed to that and is waiting for me a little ways off. I believe that we should call him to come join us. Why don't you talk to him? Please, Sister Martha! I have said what I needed to say. Also, I should not stay here while you are talking to my papa. If you allow me, I'll join Elise. I promised that I would see her after I had visited with you and talked to you." Susanne quickly turned and went to the other end of the garden, where Elise was picking weeds from the potato patch.

Sister Martha slowly went and looked out the gate. She noticed Franz, who was quietly standing outside. His back was turned, but he must have heard the sound of her steps, as he turned around to face her. She opened the gate. Slowly, he approached. His eyes were questioning, hopeful, and loving at the same time. Her steps grew faster, and he stretched out his arms to enfold her in a firm, warm embrace. She did not resist.

"I love you, Martha," he whispered.

Her eyes mirrored what he felt. "I love you too, Franz."

His smile deepened. "What I am doing here is not written in the rules of this house, Martha." He lifted her into his arms, placing her on the bench beside him, and kissed her tenderly. "Are you willing to leave this house and come into my house, Martha, and be my wife? This is a big decision and a big change in your life. Am I asking too much?"

"Oh, Franz, I have thought so much and prayed, and my answer is very clear in my heart and in my mind. I want to be with you; I am ready for my life with you. I love you, and I want to be a mother to your children too." She was in wonder at her own passion as she clung to him, and as they embraced, time and space were forgotten.

Susanne related her conversation with Sister Martha to Elise. "Yes, I wanted to get to know Sister Martha better. I know that my father loves her. She is such a kind, loving person. I am glad that I finally met her."

Elise grinned. "And that's exactly why I left. I wanted you to have privacy and see for yourself. I know that she is wonderful. She has helped me to feel better here. She is teaching me, and even if I have entirely different opinions than the others, she tolerates them. We have talked a lot together. You know, I asked her some questions about her life. It turns out that she came here at the wish of her parents. She did not even want to come here! I was shocked! I tell you; nobody would do that to me! And so I asked her whether this was the way she wanted to live, whether she was happy. Well, she is not! She said she was a nun. So what! I told her that life can change and that we are the ones who have to make our own choices. And I believe that she is thinking a lot about all that..."

Elise stopped short and looked across the garden as a big grin spread over her face. "Susanne! She has done her thinking! I believe that she has made her decision too."

Susanne's glance followed Elise's. She saw her father in a close embrace with Sister Martha. She jumped up with unconcealed delight. "Yes!" she shouted. "I knew it! I knew it could happen!" She grabbed Elise and whirled her around. "Thank you, thank you, thank you! You have helped to make it happen! You have talked to Sister Martha!"

The shouts startled Franz and Sister Martha. They saw the two girls jumping with glee. Franz motioned them to come over. "Susanne, you may have guessed it already. Martha will be your new mother."

Susanne waved away the comment and laughed. "Oh my dear papa, I knew that when I talked to Sister Martha. I am so happy that I will have Sister Martha as my mom, and I want you both to be very happy!"

Sister Martha looked at Elise. "Ever since you came here my life has been a whirlwind of change!" She looked happier than Elise had ever seen her.

"I am so happy for both of you," Elise said with sincerity. She did not comment that she would miss Sister Martha, as she did not want to put a shadow of sadness into this day. Also, she reminded herself, she had told Sister Martha about changes in life, and this applied to her own life as well. She felt a strong conviction that she would not be staying here much longer.

*M*idafternoon there was silence in the common room on an early summer day. It was interrupted by the scrape of a chair. Mother Antonia rose, cleared her throat, and prepared to make an announcement to the group. "Dear Sisters, I wanted to let you know about an important event in this house. You know our young postulant Josepha. She has been staying here for some time now, and I want to propose that it is time for her to take her vows this Sunday as a novice."

There was a short murmur of voices, then a short gasp from Josepha. She stared at the speaker. Her face was pale, and her eyes betrayed her sense of distress.

"What is it, Josepha?" asked Mother Antonia. "This is going to be a wonderful celebration for you!"

Josepha felt herself go numb with fear. Her eyes glanced across the room to where Elise was sitting. Elise's clear eyes seemed to infuse her with strength and encouragement, and she rose slowly from her chair and pushed it aside. "No, Mother Antonia," she declared loudly and clearly.

Mother Antonia stared at her in disbelief. "What do you mean?" Her voice rose in overt disapproval.

Josepha felt her body go tight, like a spring, and felt ready to bolt. "I am not taking my vows, Mother Antonia. I am not ready for a promise that I cannot keep. Also, I am leaving the convent. I want—"

Mother Antonia's voice was like a whip as it cut her short. "This is unheard of…simply outrageous! You are not supposed to act like this. It is the wish of your parents. Your behavior is a disgrace! I am appalled! Go to your room and repent!"

Josepha's eyes had lost their soft and placid look. They now held a look of resolve and fierce determination. She stepped forward in a quick motion. "I told you I'm leaving. I mean it. It is my decision." She whirled around, her long skirt streaming behind her, and ran out of the room and out of the house. Slamming the gate behind her, she ran like her life depended on it.

Even though she was barefoot, she ignored the rough road. She looked back in panic, but nobody was following her. As she slowed her steps to a steady trot, she followed the road, with her heart pounding. *Just a bit longer, just another mile*, she willed herself to continue. Out of breath she arrived at the familiar house of her aunt and knocked at the door. Swift steps came down the stairs inside, and her aunt opened the door. It felt like the door to another chapter of her life had opened.

Her aunt put her arms around the girl. "Come in, and welcome home, Josepha." Josepha felt the events of the afternoon catch up with her. Despite the relief she felt, she burst into tears as she sank into the arms of her aunt.

*A*fter Josepha's outburst and disappearance, glacial silence filled the room. Mother Antonia looked around and observed the reactions around her. Some faces showed surprise, some outrage that mirrored her own. A few looked on with a note of silent approval, even admiration, but nobody uttered a word. Mother Antonia noted that Elise's face showed no reaction. It seemed that she had deliberately put on a blank mask in order to not reveal her feelings. Mother Antonia pointedly looked at her, but the girl refused to meet her glance and turned away her head.

Anger boiled in Mother Antonia. She would deal with this young girl in privacy. Avoiding her gaze was like a silent confession that Elise knew about Josepha's plans. She recalled the frequent talks she had observed between the two girls. After a long time, Mother Antonia spoke up. "Elise, I want you to come to my study. I have some questions for you."

Elise followed her without any comment. She knew that she had to stand and answer, and she looked at Mother Antonia, unafraid. "You had questions for me, Mother Antonia?"

The clear, fearless eyes instilled even more anger in Mother Antonia. "Yes," she replied with ill-concealed emotion.

Elise noticed that Mother Antonia's eyes seemed to pierce her. She was ready to fight.

"I want you to tell me what happened to Josepha. You and she had talks together. It was obvious to me. I have reason to believe that you have influenced her in the most undue fashion. She has changed. She never had it in her to be rebellious and defiant. Speak!"

Elise looked back calmly. "I have not done anything wrong. All I have done is asked Josepha how long she had been here and whether she was happy here. She told me that she was here because her parents had decided she should live here. I did not ask much more. But she told me that she was unsure that she would stay; she was not sure that this was the life she wanted."

Mother Antonia's voice rose, "Enough! And I am certain that you encouraged her to think more about it. This is exactly what I mean. You have turned a calm, quiet girl into a rebel."

Elise took a deep breath. "Thinking is not something that makes anybody a rebel. And I do not believe that Josepha is a rebel because she is thinking for herself. She is simply growing up and having thoughts about life and what it means to her and what she wants out of it. She also does not only think about it but dares to talk about it. But maybe it is her daring to speak up that you perceive as rebelliousness."

Mother Antonia gulped for air. The very nerve of this girl to lead a conversation like that! She waved her hand. "It is better for you to leave right now. This is enough. I don't need to hear any more, but I'll deal with all of that later. You will hear from me." It was meant to sound like a threat, but Mother Antonia noticed, to her dismay, that Elise's eyes remained fearless. She seemed to be unimpressed and certainly unrepentant as she left the room.

Elise looked for Sister Martha. She had to confide in her what had happened. She found her, her hands busy, as always, with some housework. Sister Martha looked at the young face, which looked stormy. "Something has happened to you," she observed. She halted briefly then continued. "I have to confide to you that something has happened to me too."

Elise tilted her head and looked at Sister Martha curiously. "So are we both in a similar situation? Tell me what happened, Sister Martha. I mean, if you want to."

Sister Martha gave Elise a long look. "It is no secret to you that Franz and I are very much in love."

"Yes, I know, and I think it is wonderful."

Sister Martha continued. "It means that I will be leaving the convent. Franz is waiting for me to be ready. I have been doing some work here over the last few weeks, some cleaning and some preparations, so one of the sisters can take over and will find everything in good order. It is almost done. Franz has come by every evening to see me. I am preparing to go with him today. I still have to speak to Mother Antonia. She will be scandalized, of course, but I am at the point where I do not fear any reprimand, not from her, not from anybody. God created man and woman, and being in love is not a sin. It will hurt when I have to leave you behind."

Elise hugged Sister Martha. "Sister Martha, you are not the only one who will be leaving. Mother Antonia knows that I am behind the fact that Josepha ran away today. She is angry at me. She accused me of turning Josepha into a rebel, and it is clear to me that she wants to get rid of me. She said that I would hear from her. That tells me enough." Both remained silent in mutual understanding.

After a long time, Elise went back to the common room to the piano. The room was empty. She started to play, needing something that would lift her spirits. It was also her private good-bye to the room, to the instrument. The music calmed her. Her naturally bubbly personality returned as she broke into a lively movement of a Mozart sonata. It was impossible to stay glum with the trills and runs of this energizing, life-affirming music.

Outside a man was walking in deep thought, his head lowered and his hands in his pockets. His eyes were somber, and his hair was windblown. Strains of piano music floated through the open windows into the late afternoon. He had walked here often ever since his doctor had told him that taking the healing waters in Heiligenstadt, living in the country, and going for walks to enjoy nature would be good for him to get well.

He stopped to listen closely. Lately he had found that his hearing was causing him problems. It distressed and frightened him. There was ringing in his ears, but he could clearly discern that somebody was playing a piece by Mozart, probably one of his early piano sonatas. He admired the composer and was sad about the untimely death of this great man. But his music was so alive, especially the way it was being played here!

At the same time, he had to wonder. He was walking past a convent, not exactly the place where pieces of worldly music like this one were in high demand. He thought that music seemed to break through all barriers. It should not just be confined to the courts of nobility; it was there for all people. And here it was obvious that somebody felt free enough to play a nonsacred piece within the walls of a convent. A free spirit! A slight smile brightened his previously somber face. He felt a sense of kinship with the musician, as he found the boundaries of convention too restrictive for his own taste. He inhaled the brisk, refreshing evening breeze, which reflected the mood of the moment, as he continued his walk.

M other Antonia paced in her study. The events of this afternoon were upsetting her. She sighed when there was a knock at her door. Sister Martha announced a visitor to her. She was not really in the frame of mind for any visitor, but it was her sister, Lady Lichnowsky. She welcomed her and invited her to sit down.

The two sisters were total opposites: Lady Lichnowsky was a lively woman of worldly refinement and elegance, and Mother Antonia was an austere woman who had secluded herself from the world. Mother Antonia called for Sister Martha to prepare some coffee. She wanted her sister to enjoy some special refreshment, and she herself felt ready for something indulgent after the tumultuous afternoon.

The lively eyes of Lady Lichnowsky observed her sister with interest. "It is time that I came to see you, my dear sister! It has been a long time. As you know, my husband's commitments are copious. We also have houseguests and many social events."

Mother Antonia knew. She could not relate to the social life of her sister and this part of the family, but she nodded in agreement. "I know, we are all leading busy lives, everyone according to his or her fashion. The last time you heard from me was a few months back, when I needed help, as we had a young girl in our care that had been running into the road and got hit by a cart. I am very thankful to you for sending your physician."

"Ah, yes, I remember. I hope that he was of help."

"Yes," Mother Antonia replied curtly. "She recovered. She is helping Sister Martha with the domestic chores."

Lady Lichnowsky took a small sip of coffee. "There is something that is of concern to me, Antonia. My husband has a friend in Vienna, a musician and a very gifted man. Unfortunately the man has health problems. Our doctor has seen him and recommended a stay in the country."

"Will we have to look after him?" Mother Antonia questioned.

"No, there is no need for that, but all the same, it is a difficult situation. You see, when he is in Vienna, we can be of assistance, but since he is living here in Heiligenstadt, we are a good hour away by coach. He is staying near the village to give the mineral waters a try. Even a quiet stay in the country will restore his health." She paused. "I went to call on him earlier today, as I was coming out here to visit you. I dropped in just to see how he was doing. And—*Mon Dieu!*—I almost fainted when I saw his place."

She fanned herself with a lace handkerchief and moaned. "Granted, he is an artist, but this was too much! The place is in shambles and chaos. Nothing is cleaned up. It is an embarrassment if anybody comes to call. This place is not fit for human habitation!"

"What about a housekeeper? That should solve the problem," Mother Antonia interjected.

Her sister rolled her eyes. "That's just it! There *was* a housekeeper, but for some reason or other she left. Just like that—gone! Things cannot go on like that. I wanted to ask whether you would not be able to send a capable young lady, maybe a young postulant, to take charge of this household. Now, I do not know the reasons for the sudden departure of his previous housemaid. I do know that he is a very strong-willed individual. He lacks social graces and can be moody and abrupt. Some of our friends don't find him very sociable, but we all agree that he is a wonderful composer and an outstanding musician. And you should have heard some of his concerts…"

Mother Antonia's face grew animated. "I believe that I know exactly what can be done! The very same girl who was nursed back to health here, the one who was treated by your physician, Dr. Malfatti, is currently a helper here and would be an absolutely perfect match for this household. She is competent and quick. Sister Martha has noticed that she is a hard worker and able to work very efficiently on her own, without further instructions. She loves music and plays the piano very well. Besides all that, she is intelligent and educated."

Lady Lichnowsky shook her head in amazement. "She sounds like a gem! Why on earth would you want to part with her?"

Mother Antonia leaned back with a sour smile. "Of course, this all sounds too good to be true! Yes, you may as well know what has been going on here! This girl is a free spirit, and she goes against anything that is expected from a sheltered young lady. She has strongly disagreed to even become a postulant. She questions and reasons, has no qualms about speaking her mind, and she is strong willed.

"Today was the last straw. One of our postulants declared that she would not take her vows. She refused and insisted that she had a right to live her own life. When I told her that she was to take her vows, she had the gall to run out of the room and away from here. Scandalous! These two were talking to each other, and I am certain that it is due to the nefarious influence of this rebel that we have lost a postulant. And only God knows whether her influence has gone even further than this and has infected the minds of others. I have had a terrible afternoon, and I am still upset now. All this has given me a splitting headache!"

Lady Lichnowsky looked at her sister and seemed to find these revelations more entertaining than disturbing. She knew the old-school attitude of her sister, which differed from her own way of thinking. Of course there would be an instant collision course between this girl and Antonia! She was not surprised. "Well, my dear sister, this sounds like a heaven-sent solution to both of our problems, don't you think?" She looked up and listened to the strains of a piano sonata that drifted across the hallway. "What beautiful music! You have a talented player in your midst."

Mother Antonia's smile had an acrid note. "Not for much longer, if you want to take this girl, Elise, with you right now. Also you would contribute greatly to my peace of mind and to the restoration of the peace of this house. We have no use for revolutionaries."

Lady Lichnowsky smiled politely. "I will meet Elise and have a quick talk with her. Adieu for now, and thank you for your help, Antonia."

Quietly Lady Lichnowsky opened the door to the common room and listened to the music. She let Elise finish. Elise stood up and gently closed the instrument. She turned and saw the visitor. "Are you looking for anybody, and can I help you?"

"Yes, I am looking for Elise. I am Antonia's sister, Lady Lichnowsky."

"Oh, good evening! I am Elise."

The lady looked at the girl. She did not look like the fiery, revolutionary rebel her sister had described. But at the same time, she also noted that this individual was not one of the meek, submissive creatures that Antonia seemed to favor. She was of medium stature, carried herself upright, and radiated energy. Lady Lichnowsky liked what she saw. This girl would be able to stand up to a cantankerous, moody person, and she was certainly not somebody who looked timid. "I am truly pleased to meet you, and I wanted to ask you for your help. My family has a friend here in the neighborhood. He is alone and needs a housekeeper. Antonia told me that you are capable and hardworking. She recommended you for the work."

Elise was silent for a few moments. She seemed to consider this piece of news carefully. "I think it would be best if I came with you right now. I believe it would help your sister too." Without saying anything further, she walked with the visitor along the hallway.

Lady Lichnowsky gave Elise a short and critical glance. The girl looked pretty and seemed to keep herself clean. It was just incredible how neglected her clothing was! It was not dirty, but it looked threadbare and mended, like the dress of a beggar. Why would anybody do this to a girl like her? She knew how thrilled her own teenage daughters were with nice accessories, even if they were just small hairpins or an inexpensive piece of glass jewelry. Young girls liked pretty things! And this young person had nothing at all, not even a decent everyday dress.

Lady Lichnowsky shook her head: Antonia seemed to have lost all connection to the world after embracing life in the convent. Lady Lichnowsky thought of the dresses that her own daughters wore. Why, even the housemaids at her place were better dressed than this girl!

"Tell me, Elise, is there another dress you could wear? This one looks kind of worn. It won't last much longer."

Elise shook her head. "I am afraid not. I was brought here after I was hit on the road, and it seems I only wore a white gown. I was unconscious…They gave me this one, and it's the only one I have got."

Lady Lichnowsky stopped and went back to see her sister. She could not suppress a trace of irony in her question. "Dear sister, would it be possible, perhaps, to give this girl a dress that is still useable for some time? This one seems to be falling apart. I believe that giving her a dress would be in the true sense of charity, wouldn't you agree?"

Mother Antonia's face turned pink. "We are in a convent, where we are not subject to the whims of fashion or vanity."

Her sister gave her a mild but mocking look. "I am not talking about fashion, nor does this have anything to do with vanity, dear sister. I am simply looking at the practical aspects of a young person's basic needs. She is not a beggar and has a right to some dignity.

"I agree with you that I should take her with me to a more suitable workplace. She does not seem to fit in here due to her attitude. And so I hope that this will eliminate your headache and that you will have a very pleasant evening."

Mother Antonia called for Sister Martha. "Elise needs something to wear to start at her new workplace. Apparently her clothes are getting worn."

Sister Martha silently went to the linen storage to look for a suitable garment. She handed one to Elise. "Oh, Elise, it hurts to say good-bye." There were tears in her eyes.

Elise gave her a quick hug and whispered, "Remember, we both are leaving. Be happy, Sister Martha! Franz is waiting for you." She quickly turned and left with Lady Lichnowsky.

⁓

*A*fter they left, Sister Martha methodically prepared everything in the kitchen. The sisters would need their breakfast in the morning. She pulled out the plates and bowls and set them out on the table. She cut up the bread. The water buckets were full. Everything was done, but one thing would be different: they would be starting the morning without her.

Sister Martha listened as Mother Antonia's steps sounded in the hallway. There was an air of victory as Mother Antonia stood at the kitchen door. "Elise is gone." A note of satisfaction was in her voice.

"Yes," Sister Martha replied shortly.

Mother Antonia continued. "Well, there will be another helper for you."

Sister Martha looked up. "I think that you will need more than just a helper. My work is done." Silent tension hung in the air.

"Done? That does not make sense! Your work is done? How so?" Mother Antonia's voice was almost a shriek.

"I am leaving now, this evening. My work here is done, but there is other work waiting for me. There is a man who loves me, and I love him with all my heart. His three children need a mother. This will be my work from now on."

Mother Antonia stood still, like she had turned into stone. She gasped and struggled for words. "This is…this simply cannot be true! Have you lost your mind? What got into you? You are one of the sisters. What you are doing is scandalous. After fourteen years…"

Sister Martha stepped closer. Her voice was firm but calm. "Mother Antonia, have you forgotten the conversation we had a few months ago about Elise? You mentioned that people could change their minds. You also stated that you have seen persons older than young girls change their minds. I am one of those persons."

This statement left Mother Antonia without further ammunition. She was speechless. These had been her very own words when they had discussed Elise's refusal to become a postulant, and there was nothing that she could say.

Sister Martha went on. "Yes, I have been here for fourteen years, half of my life. My parents decided—against my will—that I should live my life in a convent. So I have tried to be obedient, and I have given it everything I can. But I also realized that my yearning to be a mother, to have a family, never went away, no matter how hard I tried to let it go. I do not expect you to fully understand, but please, don't let us part with bitterness and insults. All I want to do is say my good-byes in peace."

There was a quick flash of anger in Mother Antonia's face. "It all started with Elise!" Her eyes scrutinized Sister Martha's. She saw no anger, no distress, but a calm happiness that stopped her from saying more. "Good-bye, Sister Martha. This is hard for me, but I have to accept it. May God bless you."

Franz was standing beside his cart and had been waiting for Sister Martha. He helped her onto the seat beside him. The horse fell into a swift trot. Sister Martha did not look back. She looked at Franz, saw his loving face, and felt his arm wrapped protectively around her shoulders. She felt that she had been blessed more than she had ever imagined.

Franz embraced her fervently. "Martha, you are a blessing in my life." They sat in a tight embrace and forgot the world. Even though Franz did not hold the reins of the horse, the animal trotted along the familiar road, and the cart bumped along the cobblestones, taking them to his house and to their life together.

Six

The Stranger That Is No Stranger

*E*lise sat beside Lady Lichnowsky as the chaise rolled along the road to her new place of work. The countess observed Elise with lively interest. The girl seemed to be undisturbed by the sudden change of her workplace. She appeared to be more curious than apprehensive, and the countess was pleased.

"From what my sister told me, it seems that you belong out in the world and not in a convent," said Lady Lichnowsky. "I hope that this new environment will be good for you. My friend is a musician, and it occurred to me that you might enjoy working for him. Do not feel too overwhelmed or discouraged by the household that you are about to work in. It is…hm…not something that is orderly or clean." She paused, searching for the right words to describe it.

"Do you mean something like a mess or a pigsty?" Elise blurted out. Oh goodness! She probably had said something unfitting or "improper for a girl" again.

The countess laughed out loud. This girl had no fear of describing things exactly the way they were. "You are certainly very direct, and this is refreshing! Nevertheless, I would not recommend that you voice this opinion to your employer. He could find it upsetting."

"No, I won't! I'm sorry that I was very blunt about that! But I'll clean up the place. People should live in a house, not in a barn."

Lady Lichnowsky nodded in agreement. "I think that you have been taught well by Sister Martha. You may miss her."

A shadow went over Elise's face. "Yes, but then she will be leaving the convent today as well. So it is just as well that I am starting somewhere new."

Lady Lichnowsky raised her eyebrows in surprise. "She is leaving? Today? After all these years? She is a nun! This sounds incredible to me."

Elise shrugged her shoulders. "Her parents wanted her to be a nun. It was not her idea! Of course she wants to leave! She is getting married. She wants a family."

The countess gasped. "I can just imagine the state Antonia will be in." She leaned back into her seat cushion and thought this probably was Elise's doing. Maybe she *was* the revolutionary, as Antonia had described her—at least in a convent. In any event, it only confirmed in her mind that Elise was the right candidate for her new workplace. After all, Lady Lichnowsky's friend was as direct and unconventional as his new housekeeper.

The chaise stopped in front of a farmhouse outside the village. They stepped down, and the lady went up the steps to the arched doorway and pulled the doorbell. There was silence. She knocked at the door and rang again. A neighbor's door opened, and an older, grandmotherly woman stuck her head out. "Oh, Lady Lichnowsky, you are looking for your friend? He just came back, and I think he went to the back of the house, where he cannot hear the doorbell too well." She raised her voice. "Mr. Ludwig! Mr. Beethoven! Are you there? The countess has returned to see you!"

Elise's eyes opened wide. *Mr. Ludwig…Mr. Beethoven…*the shout of the woman still echoed in her ears. This was more incredible than anything else that had ever happened to her before. She had been whisked back into the year 1802 in Heiligenstadt. And, of course, Ludwig van Beethoven was living in Heiligenstadt during that year. What was she doing here at the house where he lived?

In the back a door opened, and a man with dark, disorderly hair and a sun-tanned complexion came out of the house. Elise looked into his face. It could not be called a particularly good-looking face, but it was an arresting young face that radiated restless vitality and had eyes that were dark and pondering.

Elise recognized him instantly. This was the man she had seen before, when she and Sister Martha had been gathering herbs in the field. He was the stranger who had crossed their path, to whom she had offered half of the spring flowers she had picked. She had thought then that his face looked familiar, but she had been unable to remember where she had seen it. Of course! This was Ludwig van Beethoven. She had seen a picture of the young Beethoven in one of her music-history books.

Lady Lichnowsky smiled at her friend. "My dear friend Ludwig! As I mentioned to you earlier today, I was determined to find a housekeeper for you. I went and called on my sister, Antonia, the mother superior at the convent near Saint Michael's Church. She recommended Elise as a good worker."

Elise's heart skipped a beat or two. Here was Ludwig van Beethoven, and she had been thrown into the role of being his housekeeper! Thank heavens that Sister Martha had initiated her in all the work that she needed to know.

LUDWIG VAN BEETHOVEN 1804

Beethoven's dark eyes scrutinized Elise, and there was a glint of recognition and a smile in them. "Well, this is certainly a surprise, my dear friend. It is very thoughtful of you. I accept your suggestion."

The countess seemed pleased. "Very well then. I will leave Elise here. She will be able to live in the small chamber, where your previous helper was accommodated, as she will not be returning to the convent." Lady Lichnowsky pointed toward the door. "Head inside and just up the stairs, Elise. It's a small room, but at least it is your own. I'm leaving now, but I trust that you'll do your work well."

Elise clutched the small bundle containing her dress and nightclothes she had received from Sister Martha. "Thank you, Lady Lichnowsky." The countess gave her an encouraging smile. "Good bye Elise. In time I will probably meet you again." "Good bye, Lady Lichnowsky. Have a good trip to Vienna." Turning to Beethoven, she said, "I'll be back down right away."

She opened the door and recoiled. So this was the mess the countess had mentioned! The windowpanes were blinded with dust that must have accumulated for some time. A few spiders scurried away. She hurried up the stairs to the room that would be hers. Old, stale-smelling bed linen lay around. She would rather sleep on a bare straw mattress than on a dingy bed with dirty sheets! But at least this was her space for now. Cleaning it up would have to wait till tomorrow. There was no time to do anything right now, as she was expected downstairs. Quickly she went down the stairs.

Her new employer stood in the living room, bent over a desk, which was not far from a grand piano that occupied the middle of the room. His pen flew over a page, and Elise recognized that he was writing on a music score. He quickly looked up and acknowledged her presence. "So, your name is Elise?"

"Yes. And you are Mr. Beethoven."

He looked up. "You remembered my family name rather quickly. That is surprising! Everybody here finds it unusual. Yes, it is Beethoven. I am not from here. It's a name from my ancestors. They came from the area around Ghent. So just call me Mr. Ludwig. It will be easier."

"Very well, Mr. Ludwig."

"I seem to recall that we briefly met before. You and a nun were out on a field path, gathering herbs. This may have been about two months ago. It was nice of you to share some spring flowers. So you are a postulant at the convent?"

Elise shook her head. "No, I was taken in after a cart on the road hurt me. One of the sisters nursed me back to health, but I did not want to become a postulant."

"And so you were sent to work here? Will you like that better?" His tone was skeptical.

Elise looked straight at him. "I don't know yet," she replied with disarming honesty. "I haven't even been here for an hour. I guess in time I'll find out!"

He was perplexed at this quick-witted answer. His lips curled into a smile, and he thought he had just received the only fitting reply to his inappropriate question. Indeed, how could anybody know whether a new workplace was the right choice after less than an hour!

"Maybe it is time for some supper," he suggested, pointing to the kitchen.

Elise entered the kitchen. This was not Sister Martha's clean-scrubbed domain. It was not as bad as her upstairs room, but it was certainly not a show-case of proper housekeeping or outstanding cleanliness. She looked around. It was not much different than the kitchen at the convent, just smaller: there was the wood stove, shelves with dishes, some pots and pans, and a storage pantry. There was a coffee machine on the counter, and she touched it inquisitively. Sister Martha had shown her how to prepare coffee for the mother superior or the visiting guests, and this piece looked exactly the same, like the ancient pieces she had seen on a trip to the museum. She would find her way around.

The fire in the stove was still glowing, and she quickly fanned it up and added some wood. There were some potatoes in a basket. They would have to do. She rummaged around. It did not look like a kitchen that saw a lot of use, but she found some eggs. Cautiously she cracked one open. The smell made her wrinkle her nose. Disgusting, this one was rotten! No wonder! It was summer, and nothing could be kept fresh. Luckily a few other eggs were still useable. She found a large cast-iron pan and started to prepare a simple meal. She put the fried eggs and potatoes on a plate and carried the food over to the table.

"Here is some supper for you, Mr. Ludwig."

He looked up from his writing, silently went to the table, and sat down. "You are certainly fast with your work," he commented. "What about your evening meal?"

Elise sensed that he was a solitary individual. This was not a place where everybody sat down together at a big table like at the convent. "I'll eat something in the kitchen," she responded. A short nod was his only answer. It seemed to be a suitable arrangement for him. She sat at the kitchen table with her share of the evening meal. All of a sudden she felt very much alone. She missed Sister Martha.

Later she quietly stepped back into the room. He was back to working at his desk, writing by the light of two dim candles, but the plate was empty. He paused a moment and said, "This was good. I don't think you have more work today. I do not start the day too early, and I'm not somebody who wants much for breakfast. But I appreciate my coffee."

"I will be up early enough for my work, good night." With this, she turned, took a small oil lamp, and went up the stairs to the room under the roof as the flickering light cast her shadow on the wall. She crawled onto the straw mattress and curled up. It had been an eventful day, with Josepha running away, herself being sent away from the convent, and Sister Martha leaving there too. Elise was supposed to work for a stranger, and yet the stranger was not unknown to her, as she had played his music and had read about his life. The confusing part was that she had done all that in 2002, and now she was back in 1802, a time that was not that well known to her.

This was all very bewildering, but somehow it was becoming an exciting adventure for her. Even the coarse mattress did not bother her, and as she drifted off into sleep, she knew that tomorrow would be the start of something new and unknown. The thought did not bother her. There was a common denominator to life, no matter which century: there were turns and twists and changes. She would treat it like a book and take it one page at a time.

The next morning, Elise awoke to the crowing of a rooster. It was dawn. She was used to starting her days early, and she looked curiously out of the tiny window. From the small window she saw the road in front of the farmhouse that widened into a small square where a fountain bubbled. A farmer was driving a pushcart toward the open fields. Quickly she got dressed, combed her hair, and twisted it into a bun, the way Josepha had shown her how to do it. She thought of Josepha and of Sister Martha, and she was happy for both of them. She felt a split second of uncertainty. What about her? What was in her future? She shook off the notion. She would have to wait and see… For now it was time to go downstairs and see her new environment.

Somewhere a church clock struck six times. Elise tiptoed into the room where her employer had been working yesterday. Everything was quiet, and the room was empty. Obviously he was still asleep. This suited her rather well. She went into the kitchen and looked for the water buckets and walked out of the house. At the fountain in the little square opposite the house, several women were filling their water jugs and buckets. They were engaged in a lively chat and eyed her curiously as she approached. She said, "Good morning," and they appeared to be a friendly group.

One of them was the older woman that had opened the door yesterday and had shouted for Mr. Beethoven. She gave Elise an encouraging smile. "Are you the new housekeeper of Mr. Ludwig?"

"Yes, I arrived here yesterday."

"I am Moser-Marie, your neighbor. Mr. Ludwig rented half of our house for this summer."

"My name is Elise. I was sent over from the convent to work for him. I have worked with one of the sisters there, and the mother superior thought that it would be better if I worked here." She filled her buckets and prepared to leave.

The older woman joined her. "I hope that he is treating you well."

Elise gave her a questioning glance and said, "I was told that his previous housemaid left without any notice."

"Ah, yes," Moser-Marie sighed. "She was not too bright, I'm afraid, but then he is not easy to deal with either. Everything has to be just so. Imagine, his last housekeeper reported that he threw a fit if she did not count out exactly sixty coffee beans for his cup of morning coffee! Once he threw an egg at her, because he said that it was not fresh. And she had to write everything in a book, every penny she spent at the market. And if things did not add up, he would fly off his handle! Sometimes he walks through the neighborhood without even saying hello to anybody. It seems that he is just different, but I guess that's what you get with an artist! You know that he is a musician from Vienna?"

"Yes, I heard that he is a great musician," Elise replied, "but I did not hear all the other details." She could not suppress a grin. This man sounded like a piece of work!

Moser-Marie patted her on the shoulder. "Listen, you did not hear these details from me, right?"

Elise put a deliberately dim-witted expression on her face and held her hand to her ear. "What details?"

Moser-Marie looked at her and laughed out loud. "You are funny! Listen, if you need to know anything, just ask. I'm usually home, and I help my husband with candle making. Joseph is a beekeeper. He is out all day."

Elise's mind raced…there were so many things she needed to know! Where would she get everything for their daily needs? "Yes, there is one question I have right now. Where do I go to buy things like bread or meat or vegetables?"

Moser-Marie understood. "Oh, you were in the convent. No wonder you don't know your way around here! Just go down the road. It is just a few minutes from the house. There is a market every morning, and you will find most everything. And if you just need a few eggs or some milk, you can buy those from me. We are keeping a goat and a few chickens, and we also have some kitchen herbs and vegetables in the yard."

"Thank you so much. This is helping me a lot." Elise waved to her and entered the house. It was still quiet. Mr. Ludwig had not exaggerated when he stated that he was not an early riser. She got the fire started in the stove and put water into the coffee machine. Thank goodness for talkative neighbors like Moser-Marie! With a mischievous smirk on her face, she counted out exactly sixty coffee beans and deliberately lined them up neatly beside the old coffee mill, like a small army of soldiers that were ready to fight an early morning battle. That should prevent any morning tempests from his side.

She found it hard to believe that she would have to deal with such a controlling, ill-tempered individual. But she also remembered something about her own grandfather. As he had become older, he had become hard of hearing. With the hearing loss, he had also become deeply distrustful of people around him—even his own family—grumpy, and difficult to please. Yes, of course it was known that Beethoven suffered hearing loss, and even though he was a young man, he would probably feel similarly: the struggle to understand and feeling misunderstood were not easy to take. She cut a few slices of bread and found some butter, which she placed on the table.

There was a shuffling of feet in the room next door. Somebody seemed to be waking up. After a short while Elise's new employer entered the living area. He appeared carefully dressed, and even the wild mane of hair had a semblance of order. He paced around and watched what Elise was doing with interest. "I believe that I mentioned I don't want much for breakfast?"

"Yes, I remembered that." She pointed to the bread and butter.

"What about my coffee?" He peered into the kitchen and scanned the worktable, spotting the coffee machine. "Just don't make some horrible brew! I want—"

Elise pointed to the beans. "I hope that is the right amount."

His eyes flew over the lineup of beans, and he looked surprised and puzzled. "Looks perfect to me. How on earth…" He left the sentence unfinished. Obviously he was perplexed, wondering how anybody could measure out the correct amount of coffee without even asking.

Elise did not offer any comment but remained silent, prepared the coffee, and placed it on the table. She felt a wicked sense of satisfaction: *that's one and oh for me! Try to throw a temper tantrum now, mister,* she thought.

"I'll be out for the morning." He grabbed his hat from the coatrack and prepared to leave.

"I am afraid that I'll have to get some supplies for your lunch and dinner from the market," Elise remarked. With interest she watched his reaction.

His forehead furrowed, and he looked at her with distrust and suspicion. "There must be something left?" He opened the pantry door, but only empty shelves stared back at him. "Hmm, here is some money. Get a chicken for soup; get some vegetables too, a few potatoes, onions, a few eggs, and some bread. This should be enough." Carefully he counted out some coins and put them on the table.

"And if the Italian merchant is there," he added, "buy some macaroni and Parmesan cheese. Do you know at all what macaroni and Parmesan cheese is? This Italian food is relatively new to this area! Also, I want to see all the bills, and everything you buy has to be written down here, down to the last penny." He grabbed a worn book, where household expenses seemed to be listed.

Elise felt that she was being tested. He had rattled down all his requests in quick succession, very obviously expecting to see her stumped and frazzled by the list. To his surprise, he did not get this kind of reaction from her.

"Of course I know macaroni and Parmesan," she replied. "It is one of my favorites. So, you want…" Without missing anything, Elise rapidly reiterated every single item he had requested. He noted with amusement that there was a mischievous glint in her eyes. It was like a game of fencing between two sparring partners, and she was agile and ready to fight back. This was different from the previous housemaid, who worked willingly but otherwise had been slow and not too astute. This girl, Elise, was quite different! He backed off and watched her eyes, which observed him and sent out one clear message: "I am reading you." She turned to start her work as he left the house.

Seven

A Collision of Characters

*E*lise looked around the downstairs area. She had cleaned up the dishes and attacked some of the grime in the kitchen. At least this was a start! This was a bit better, but a lot more work was necessary to transform this disaster area into something that resembled a home. The living area was next. It looked untidy. Dust was on every piece of furniture, and music sheets were scattered on the windowsill, on the grand piano, and on the table. Some ripped up music sheets littered the floor under the desk. A wilted bunch of flowers stood in a glass vase on a side table, and beside the vase sat a half-empty cup of coffee, in which a few dead flies floated. She spotted a pile of unwashed clothes that were negligently thrown over the backrest of an upholstered armchair. So far so bad…

Elise saw that she had her work lined up—not just for a few hours. She pushed the door that led into the bedroom open and hurried to open the window to air out the smell of sweat and stale air.

This room was even worse than the kitchen and living room combined! Everything was grimy and dusty. Of course the bed had been left unmade. That was not even a problem, but the bed linen was really just a pile of dirty sheets. A small rag rug could have been a cozy bedside mat, but unfortunately it contained more dirt than fiber. It had an unsavory grayish-brown color, with a few stains of unknown origin. Nobody should even dare to step on that thing with bare feet!

A half-empty wineglass and a few empty bottles stood on the bedside table. Beside them lay a bundle of music sheets that looked like the rough draft to a future work. Curiously she looked at one of the sheets. It was written with tidy, punctilious notes and detailed instructions for dynamics, and this work was in sharp contrast to the sense of disorganization, mayhem, and neglect that reigned elsewhere in the household.

Elise followed tracks of dirty footprints to a closet. What a mess! There were three pairs of dirty shoes, the soles covered with mud, on the floor of the closet. Some smelly knee socks lay around to add to the untidy appearance. It was slightly overwhelming, but it did not even end there! Elise remembered her own room under the roof. She had no desire to sleep in the dirty bedsheets; she would rather just continue to sleep on a bare, scratchy straw mattress.

But she had to pace herself: first things first. First of all, she had to go to the market to get some supplies, as Mr. Ludwig would be back and want his lunch. After that she would declare war on dirt, dust, and chaos.

She grabbed a large basket that hung on a kitchen hook and pocketed the coins she had been given. It did not seem customary to lock the doors during the day. Different times! This was a village, and people seemed to watch out for each other. This feeling was confirmed when she heard a woman's voice calling out her name. She stopped and turned around and noticed Moser-Marie was leaving the other side of the house.

"Are you going to the market too?" asked Moser-Marie.

Elise nodded and waited for her. They walked along the small road.

"I hope that you won't mind if I tell you where you get the best deals," Moser-Marie said.

"No, not at all! I am thankful for your help. I know what I have to buy, but otherwise it's pretty new to me. I don't know this market."

They arrived, and quite a few stalls were set up. Moser-Marie's quick black eyes darted around. Elise couldn't help comparing this agile, wiry woman with alert eyes to a lively, chirpy, small bird. She was probably in her seventies, but age was just a number and did not seem to be a burden to her.

Moser-Marie pointed to a stall. "This is the baker with fresh bread. It's best to buy here. The other baker, across from here, sometimes brings stale loaves." They both stopped and bought a loaf of bread.

"Over here!" Moser-Marie pointed. "This is a butcher, and his prices are good. He is also honest with his weights." Elise stopped and purchased a chicken that was already cut up. They went to purchase vegetables next.

Elise looked for the Italian merchant but did not see him. Moser-Marie knew where he was. "He is the man with the donkey cart on the other side. Just go over there. Mr. Ludwig is fond of these newfangled Italian foods." Elise asked for a pound of macaroni and a piece of Parmesan cheese.

The man looked at her questioningly. *"Tu mangia* pasta?" Seeing Elise's blank look, he tried again, "You eat pasta?"

Elise shook her head: "No, no, it's for Mr. Ludwig. I keep house for him."

"Ah, *il Signor Luigi, il musico*!" He smiled broadly and jokingly blew her a kiss: *"E che bella signorina*!"

Elise shook her head and laughed. "Too many compliments!"

The merchant cut a small wedge of Parmesan and tied a small bundle of macaroni with a piece of string. Elise paid and left. She had all her purchases in the basket.

Moser-Marie was standing and waiting for her. "All finished?"

"Yes, just the eggs and a bit of milk. But I'll buy them from you."

Moser-Marie lifted her basket onto her head, and they headed back to the house. She inquired how Elise's work was going, and Elise elected not to mention the impossible condition of the household. Moser-Marie was helpful, but she also loved to chat. If Elise said anything derogatory, it could be fodder for gossip at the village fountain tomorrow or even earlier. Instead Elise simply said, "Oh, it's lots of work. Nobody has been doing any housework there for a while. So it's time to do some washing. But I better prepare lunch first."

She bought the eggs, and Moser-Marie gave her a small pitcher of milk. Elise wondered aloud, "I just don't know what he likes or whether there are things he cannot stand."

Marie smiled. "I felt sorry for him when he first moved into the house. So my husband and I invited him for our midday meal. We had roasted a chicken. I had cooked some new carrots, and he liked that well enough. I had baked a cake for dessert, but he said that he does not really care for sweets. I know that he loves fish, but they are harder to get now. It's summer, and there was nobody at the market today. Another time I gave him some bread soup, and he just about licked the bowl." She giggled at the memory.

Elise took note of all the points, and then she laughed. "Licking bowls is something I would do, but I always got into trouble for that! But I promise I will mind my manners."

Moser-Marie waved her hand. "Not to worry. I have noticed that he does not always have the best manners!" She stopped and put her hand to her heart. "But, Elise? I did not tell you this detail."

Elise laughed. "What detail, Moser-Marie?" They laughed at their private joke, waved a cheerful good-bye to each other, and parted ways.

Quickly Elise grabbed the book for the household expenses, but she stopped short. Her handwriting was different from the customary German writing of this time. This would never do! With her most meticulous printing, she entered all the items and amounts into the book. At least the numbers were identical to what she was used to. Next she hurried up with the kitchen work. The bread soup Moser-Marie had talked about was simmering on the stove. Elise prepared some salad with the greens from the market as well.

⌒⌒

*M*r. Ludwig had not returned yet, and she decided to get the washing started. The big water kettle was on the stove, and the warm kitchen turned even hotter. Elise had the windows wide open, but sweat dripped from her face. Luckily it was a warm day with a strong breeze, so the laundered items would easily dry within a few hours. She grabbed the dirty bed linen and the shirts she had found in the room and threw them in the washtub that stood outside the kitchen door. More dirty laundry followed. She scrubbed the laundry, ran for more buckets of water, and rinsed it all thoroughly—God, this was brutal work! Where was a washing machine when she needed it? To make it worse, she had to wring it all out!

Finally it was done. At least everything looked clean. The sunshine and wind should do the rest. She hung all the wash on the laundry line, where it fluttered in the warm breeze of the high-noon hour.

As the church clock in the distance struck one, the door opened, and Mr. Ludwig entered. He glanced around and went into the bedroom. With a furrowed brow, he entered the living area. "What in the devil's name are you doing here? The bed is stripped, and my clothes are gone. I can't find a thing! All I have to do is leave for a few hours, and all hell breaks loose!" He sounded irritated and ill-tempered.

Elise returned his stare. "I am washing the dirty bed linen, and I thought that it would only be fitting to wash all the other unclean clothing that was lying around in the living room and in the bedroom. Nobody has done that for a while."

He was not finished with his tirade. "Who told you to do that? Not me!"

"No, it was your friend Lady Lichnowsky. She was very clear with her request. She asked me to look after your household, as the previous house-keeper had left in a hurry. So, looking after a household includes keeping it like a house, not like a barn! You told me that you would be back around midday, so I have done the errands at the market, and I have prepared lunch for you too."

His voice grew louder. "I don't care what Lady Lichnowsky told you! I wanted somebody to look after the basic daily needs. This place does not have to be spotless. This is my home for the summer, and nobody has a right to tell me how it has to look." His fist crashed on the table and made the candlestick bounce. "Damn Lady Lichnowsky, and damn the day that she dropped you here. I never asked for it. What the hang—"

Elise stepped forward. Her eyes were flashing, and she was furious. "Is this how you talk about your friends? Well, that is just lovely! You may be a famous musician, but that does not give you the right to act like an ill-behaved, overgrown brat!"

"How dare you—"

"Oh, yes, I dare! You are a human who deserves to live in human conditions and not in an animal stable. Besides you certainly have other friends beside the Lichnowskys who will come to visit you here. Do you really want to embarrass yourself totally? What will they think? I'll tell you exactly what they will think! They'll come here, see the mess you are living in, and then they'll leave, roll their eyes, and gossip just like this, 'Yes, and just imagine I visited the famous Ludwig van Beethoven! You won't believe what I saw! I just about threw up when I saw his pigsty of a summer residence in Heiligenstadt! Summer residence, my foot! This was not fit for a person to live in! He should get himself a housekeeper.'"

After this tumble of words, Elise stopped and took a breath. *Now I have done it*, she thought, *he is going to kick me out on the spot.*

There was silence. His face was a study of mixed emotions. The furious expression was gone. It was like a thunderstorm that had run its course and subsided as quickly as it started. There was amusement in his face and something like admiration. He swallowed the next comment he had wanted to make. She had put him in his place: all he had requested was done, but she had also complied with the wishes of his friend. And in a clear, merciless way, she had held an image of his home in front of him that did not look too complimentary.

His voice became quieter. "What about the money that you spent at the market? I want to see the household expenses in the book." His fingers drummed nervously and annoyingly on the table.

Elise reached for the book and handed it to him. He squinted at her writing. "This is the most peculiar writing I have seen! Why do you print it like in a book?"

"This is the way I have been taught to print at school. Everybody can read it this way. It looks different, but whoever wrote in this book before managed to make it look like chicken scratch. At least I find it hard to decipher. I expect that you can read what I wrote down?"

He sat down heavily on a chair. "Of course I can read it! It is just unusually tidy," he grumbled. He felt somewhat defeated. There was really nothing left to complain about. Carefully, almost pedantically, he counted the leftover money, one coin after the other. "I expect that you will have to make more purchases tomorrow. So I'll leave the money on the table for you. Just make sure that everything is accounted for."

As he pushed the money to the side of the table, one of the coins, a groschen, slipped out of his fingers. It rolled over the table's edge, jingled on the floor, and kept on rolling till it finally disappeared into a deep crevasse between the roughhewn wooden floorboards. He had tried to catch the coin, but it was gone. Deep in the crevasse, out of anybody's reach, it brightly glittered, like it was teasing him and mocking his effort to retrieve it. Furiously he stomped on the floor and yelled a string of colorful oaths.

Elise was standing in the kitchen, and out of the corner of her eye, she had caught a glimpse of the glittering journey of the coin. Still, she was hardly prepared for the volley of cussing and swearing that erupted. What would the neighbors think? She hurried to close the window. "Good Lord! What happened now?"

"Oh damn it all! Here I try to keep my money together, and this goddam groschen is gone! The devil can have it!" His foot crashed on the crevasse, but the coin was not about to be dislodged from its final resting place. He growled in exasperation. "These are the things that I just cannot stand! Hell and damnation!"

He took a deep breath, and next there was silence. It seemed like the outburst was over as quickly as it started. "You said that you have cooked lunch. I will gladly have some; it is late."

Elise placed the soup and the salad on the table for him and retreated to the kitchen. She was hungry too, and a cranky adult who acted like a misbehaving child would not spoil her appetite. From all appearances she had not been fired from her workplace yet.

He stood at the entrance of the kitchen, appearing a bit tamer than before. "Thank you! You managed to make one of my favorites. This was very tasty. I'll be leaving to go and take the waters at the bathhouse."

Elise stared at him in unconcealed surprise. He had said "thank you."

"Why do you look so surprised?"

Elise looked at him with an amused grin. "Oh, you just surprised me when you said 'thank you.' I did not expect that after the fit you threw before."

He shook his head, and in his dark eyes glittered a smile of amusement. "You are very direct, Elise. But I should not fault you for that, as I am very similar myself."

Elise eyed him speculatively. "I just had a thought. You were upset about the lost money before. Sometimes when I am upset, I write the upsetting event into my journal. It makes me feel better."

Her remark piqued his interest. "This sounds intriguing. I am not much of a writer. But there is one thought: I can turn it into music. That sounds like a project. Yes, I like that!" He left with a cheerful smile and whistled a tune on his way out.

*E*lise continued her work. This was harder than at the convent, as she had to do everything herself. Her bed linen was next. Eventually it would dry. Otherwise she would sleep on the straw mattress without any sheets for another night. She made up the bed in the bedroom, threw out the empty bottles, removed the coffee cup with the drowned flies, discarded the wilted flowers, and washed the floors. Next she washed the mud off the boots and put them out on the doormat to dry

When it was all done, she was bone-tired. It had been a big load of work, and she was not even finished. Everything looked a bit more orderly, but this was like a construction site in progress. She gathered the stray music sheets and placed them on the piano. The curtains were as dingy as before, and there was the bedside rug, but that was another story! There was simply not enough time in one day.

Next she would have to prepare supper and clean up afterward, and it looked like there was no end in sight. Quickly she went on another trip to the water fountain.

A neighbor greeted her. "Done with all the work for today?"

Elise offered a tired smile. "No, I still have to make supper, but after that I'm done."

"Well, good luck tomorrow—Mr. Ludwig can be glad that he finally has somebody to look after his place. I heard that he is not a pleasant person to work for."

Elise caught the lurking, probing glance of the woman, but she refused to take the bait. "It has been a good day, lots of work but good. Have yourself a good evening too." She went back, cooked some macaroni, and picked a few sprigs of basil from the small herb garden in the back.

Elise wiped her hands clean and went into the living area. Longingly, she eyed the open grand piano. She pulled up the piano bench and sat down. This was her special reward after the work was done. The last piece she had played at the convent came to her mind, the sonata by Mozart, so lively, so full of energy. She started to play, and the music drifted through the open windows into the calm evening. A feeling of energy surged back into her tired body, and she felt happy as she noticed how the music lifted up her spirits.

She did not notice the door opening as Mr. Beethoven entered. He had been walking along the street, and as he approached the house, he had heard the piano music coming from it. The person that had come to mind was Lady Lichnowsky. She loved playing the piano, but he'd dismissed the thought immediately. This was not her style of playing; this sounded like a different player. With a start, he'd recognized the piece: it was the same Mozart sonata that a person had played in the convent when he had walked by a few days ago. He now realized who was playing this piece! It must be Elise. She had been at the convent at the time; it was just before Lady Lichnowsky had brought her to his place.

Still, he could not believe it, but as he opened the door, he saw Elise at the piano, and to his amazement, she was a very accomplished pianist. On the one hand he was annoyed: here was somebody who worked at his house and had taken the liberty of playing on his instrument. His piano! On the other hand, he was intrigued how she presented this early piano piece by Mozart, and he simply could not stay angry. This was great music!

He sat down. The creaking of the chair startled her. She turned and stopped playing. "You are the first housekeeper that has played on my piano," he said seriously.

Elise bit her lip. Oh no! He was probably going to blow up again. Of course, it was his instrument, and she could understand that he felt protective of his property.

"I apologize. It was my mistake. I should have asked you first." She stood up.

"Elise, I did not mean to scold you! You are the first housekeeper here who actually plays the piano. I am amazed. You have talent."

"Thank you, Mr. Ludwig. Yes, I love music."

Elise served him his dinner. As she cleaned up later, he was again busy writing music. He looked up. "If it is enjoyable for you, feel free to play. You can use the instrument any time when I am not using it."

Elise's face brightened. "Thank you so much. This is a great privilege for me. I love playing the piano." He wished her a good night, and she went to her room.

The light of a full moon shone into her window. Her bed linen had dried. She had thrown it into a pile on the mattress and was glad that she could see well enough to make up her bed in the moonlight. Ahhh…she stretched under the covers. This felt good! The sheets smelled of a summer day. This little upstairs room was like her quiet sanctuary after a busy day. She looked outside. There was stillness. In the distance, a dog was barking. The village had gone to sleep. What would tomorrow bring? More work, of course. This household was an ongoing project. She thought that she would be able to enjoy playing the piano downstairs, and with a smile on her face, she fell asleep.

A group of women were busy at the fountain, filling their water buckets. They also shared the newest gossip of the village. "Have you heard that this musician—what's his name—has a new housekeeper? Poor thing!"

Another woman chimed in, "Oh, I can't see anybody lasting long in that place. Once I looked through the window when he was gone and—Holy Mother of God!—that place is horrible! Anybody who works for a slob like him is punished!"

Another one added, "And she looks like a young girl too. Having to put up with the temper of that man! Dreadful! I walked by yesterday at one, and I heard him shout something. One of the temper tantrums he seems to have without any warning. This is the reason why the last household helper left. It did not sound good! I bet you my bottom penny that she'll be gone as fast as she came."

Moser-Marie approached the fountain with her buckets. Immediately the questions flew around. "Moser-Marie, is the housekeeper still there, or has she taken off already? I heard him yell and carry on yesterday afternoon. She may have taken to her heels after that."

A volley of laughter from the women followed the statement. Moser-Marie's quick glance silenced the gossip. With her thumb she pointed over her shoulder. "She is obviously still there. Here she comes to get water. Why don't you ask her, if you cannot contain your curiosity? She can tell you more. It's none of my business!"

Elise had seen the group of women talking from a distance. She was pretty sure that they were talking about her. She was a new arrival here and the object of intense curiosity in a village where not much else was going on. The fact that all the conversation stopped when she arrived at the fountain only confirmed her suspicion. She smiled at the group and gave them a friendly "good morning"—but nothing else. After that she quickly went back to the house.

Moser-Marie stuck her head into the kitchen window. "Have a good day, Elise! Here is some fresh milk. No, I don't want any money for that! Just enjoy it!"

"Thank you so much! You are so kind. And thank you again for showing me around at the market yesterday!" Elise waved to her and went on with the morning chores.

Mr. Ludwig had consumed his coffee and breakfast in silence and after that had left after quickly shouting, "I'll be back at lunchtime." Elise went about her daily round of work. A quick walk to the market was first. Moser-Marie had mentioned to her that her employer was fond of goulash, a spicy meat stew. She looked for the butcher stall that she had recommended, but he was not there. Too bad! She would have to buy at the other one. She asked for a pound of cut-up beef and carefully watched as the butcher grabbed his scale and threw some cubes of meat on it. It indicated one pound, but Elise noticed that with a quick flick of his hand he removed a piece of meat before he packaged it. Of course! It would not be one pound anymore. This man was out to cheat his customers! "Hold it!" she said with a loud voice.

The man looked up with a scowl. "Why? What do you want now?"

Elise pointed to the package. "Just put this on your scales again! This isn't a pound!" A few people had gathered behind her to watch the scene.

"What? Are you calling me a cheater? Impertinent!"

"I did not call you anything," retorted Elise. "I simply asked you to put it on the scales once more."

A voice from the group shouted, "Yes, and if you are an honest man, such a request should not even bother you. Just put the package on the scales again, and everybody can see who is right!"

The man's face reddened with anger. He placed the package on the scales, and the needle indicated a quarter pound less. He ripped the package open, added the missing piece of meat, and shoved it across the table to Elise. "I don't need customers like you!" he snarled.

"You don't have to worry! I won't be back!" She paid and turned away.

A voice from the group shouted, "And nobody needs dishonest merchants like you." And someone else yelled even louder, "Listen, everybody here!

Think twice before you buy your meat here!" There was laughter and mumbles of approval, and people moved away from the stall. All the prospective customers left.

Elise hurried home, cut up the meat and onions, and put the stew on the fire. It was time for more cleaning. The food would simmer on the stove without her constantly watching over it, and she was free to take care of the next items: down with the curtains, and away with the small rug! She soaked them in a tub and was shocked. The water turned grayish-brown! Thank goodness that it was not too far to the fountain! She had to make several trips before all the dirt had been washed and rinsed out.

Mr. Ludwig seemed to have a built-in clock, as he swung open the door precisely when the church clock struck one. "Elise!"

His call brought her inside. She had just finished hanging up the curtains and the rug. The wind had picked up, and everything should be dry by evening. She gave him a quick glance. He looked as ill-tempered as he had looked exactly twenty-four hours ago. He looked like what she called "hangry," a combination of hungry and angry. This sounded like a repeat performance from the day before: temper tantrums before lunch!

"Yes, Mr. Ludwig?"

He made no effort to be civilized. "For God's sake, are you turning the house upside down every day from now on? This is intolerable! Granted, there is some dirt, but this cleaning frenzy can drive anybody crazy! I'm not willing to put up with this, you hear me?" He shouted loud enough that he could be heard from a few houses away.

Elise shook her head. "I hear you. And the way you are yelling, the entire neighborhood can hear you too, loud and clear! No, this is not what I had planned. There is enough for me to do here without the extra work. But you cannot have rags full of dirt on the windows. You could not call these things curtains anymore. And your bedside rug is beautiful. It's just a shame nobody could see the colors in it because it was so full of dirt and grime. So I washed it." She looked up quickly and continued. "It will not inconvenience you in any way, as tonight everything will be dry and back in its place."

Reasoning seemed to work, at least for now. He kicked off his boots and sat down in front of the table, but he sounded as querulous as before as he bellowed a grumpy, "Do I have any chance of getting something to eat?"

Instead of answering, Elise went to the kitchen to get the bowl with goulash and placed it on the table in front of him. She brought a basket with bread slices too and placed it on the table. Without a word he grabbed a piece of bread and bit into it. His voice rose to a shout. "Do you call this bread? This is not fresh, not the way it should be. Can't you get something better?" Angrily he hurled the bread slice at her.

Elise reacted in a split second. She caught the slice midflight and tossed it back at him. Her aim was accurate, hitting him in the chest. The slice bounced off his chest and landed in the soup bowl with a splash. The brown meat broth left a few colorful spots on his shirt and also on his face.

For a few seconds there was absolute silence. Elise prepared herself for the next outburst. Incredulously, he looked at her. "You threw the bread at me, you…"

Elise stared him down and pointed at him. "You started it, and don't you even deny it!" She tried to keep a straight face but had a hard time not bursting out into laughter: here was the famous Mr. Ludwig van Beethoven, who had thrown one of his infamous fits and wound up with spots on his shirt and face!

He stared at her, stared at his shirt, and stood up to survey the damage in a mirror. Elise waited. Would there be yet another blowup? He stood there for a few seconds, and then all of a sudden, his face dissolved into a huge grin. He recognized how ridiculous the entire situation was. He had started a fight, and she had countered it. Of course, he had not expected her to react like that, catching a missile in midair and shooting it back at him with precision! That the bread had landed in the soup bowl and left some battle marks on his face was like something straight out of a comedy. He threw back his head and shook with laughter; tears of laughter streamed down his face. As he looked up, he saw that Elise was laughing too.

Slowly he wiped the spots off his face and sat down. "I think I should try the goulash now before it gets cold." He laughed again. "And I better leave the shirt on till after lunch. I'm not the cleanest eater. It may get a few more spots."

Elise smiled. "I did not mean to get your shirt dirty or your face."

He grinned and looked slightly embarrassed. "You know, sometimes my temper just gets the best of me. I can't really blame anybody except myself. I think it is time to make peace. Why don't you sit here at the table and have your lunch too? By the way, it's very good."

Elise agreed but quickly went to the linen closet and put out a clean shirt. "Better take that off after lunch. You can't go out wearing a shirt with dots and spots all over." He smiled at her and nodded.

*T*he late-afternoon sun was hot, but a breeze made the temperature tolerable. Elise opened the windows wide, so the washed floors would dry faster. At long last she had restored some sense of pleasant order into the house. The curtains were hung up again, and the windowpanes were shiny. She stood back and looked at the rooms with a critical eye. If anybody were to come and call, the place would look like a relaxing home in the country. It was no longer a neglected, depressing residence. It reflected the cheery ambience of a place in a village, not high-strung and city-like but comfortable and earthy.

She put a checkered tablecloth on the table and placed the candlesticks back on the standing desk where Mr. Ludwig liked to work. It would be nice to go into the field and collect a bunch of summer flowers, but her work was not finished yet, as she had supper to prepare. Maybe there would be time tomorrow or even later this evening. She had another idea: the apricot tree in the backyard was loaded with golden, luscious orbs that would look wonderful on a plate. She could use them to decorate the dining table. Quickly she picked some of the fruit and arranged it on the blue-glazed plate that matched the blue-checkered tablecloth, and she was happy with the result.

Almost all the work for the day had been completed. Maybe there would be time to play her beloved piano. As she turned around, she saw Mr. Ludwig quietly standing at the kitchen door. He cast an awkward, almost apologetic glance at her and held a large bunch of summer flowers in his hands. "I gathered them on my way home. I thought that it was my turn to pick them. Last time it was you who shared a bunch of spring flowers with me. These are summer flowers. I should have done it earlier."

Elise laughed with delight. "Oh, these are so beautiful! You know, I had just thought that I should go and pick some for the table. But I ran out of time! Thank you! This is so nice of you!" She took the flowers, put them into a glass pitcher with water, and placed them on the dining table. He sat down quietly, and Elise finished her chores.

Later she sat outside on the garden bench and found that this was like a peaceful sky after a lot of thunder and lightning. As she came into the house, Mr. Ludwig looked up from his writing. "You have put a lot of effort into your work, and it shows. Thank you for all your work. Have a good night, Elise."

"Thank you. I hope that you have a good night too." She climbed up the creaky stairs to her room and curled up under the covers, which smelled of sun and fresh air. As she started to drift off into sleep, she heard piano music from downstairs, magical and soothing. This was peace after some tumultuous scenes during the day. She did not know the music, but she fell asleep with one thought: *Tomorrow! Tomorrow I will play.*

Eight

PIANO LESSONS FOR ELISE

*A*nother summer day dawned over Heiligenstadt. Life had fallen into a steady rhythm of morning work and afternoon routines for Elise. Every morning she took a quick walk to the fountain and exchanged friendly greetings with the neighbor women. There was nonverbal astonishment from their side. The new housekeeper was still there. But word had also gotten around that this girl was nobody's fool. She had been seen dealing with a dishonest butcher who wanted to cheat her out of a quarter pound of meat, and she had stood her ground, insisting that she get her money's worth. A few days later, she had given a loaf of bread back to a baker. As he handed it to her, she'd scrutinized it shortly and pointed out that there was mold on it and she would not be willing to buy stale bread.

To their consternation, neighbors had heard loud yelling on several occasions at the house where Mr. Ludwig was spending his summer. This man had a bad temper! But the same neighbors noted with surprise that the noise had settled and the place had become peaceful. Moser-Marie noticed that he had come home with a bouquet of flowers in his hand after one especially vehement tantrum, but she did not share this observation with her friends. She liked to talk, but she drew her line on gossip. Nevertheless, she resolved to speak to Elise. This girl was certainly not a pushover, but Moser-Marie was concerned about her well-being.

Elise was finishing her afternoon chores when Moser-Marie knocked at the window. Elise went outside.

"I just wanted to see how things are going for you," said Moser-Marie. "I hope that you don't perceive me as a snoop."

"No, this is fine with me," replied Elise. With a chuckle, she added, "As long as the details from here do not make the news in the village."

"Ah, no! I can promise that is not going to happen. The women asked me at one point whether you were still working here, and I told them that they should go ahead and ask you. So I want to stay out of this. The reason I am asking how you are doing is the fact that I got worried about you some time back. We heard Mr. Ludwig yell all the way at our place. My husband was prepared to come over, but it was quiet after that. We are neighbors, but we did not want to intrude. But, Elise, he is not hurting you?"

"Oh, no! I would have taken off had he tried that! He never has, but he just has a temper at times, and he shouts! Can he ever shout! But take it from me, Moser-Marie; I'm not somebody he can push around. Maybe the previous helper simply was fed up or even got scared. I don't know what happened, but he has had no luck with me. Actually, things have changed. He is very polite now, quiet but friendly."

"Well, it sounds like you are taming a lion, and you seem to have a way of doing that! Recently I saw him bring a bunch of flowers back from his walk," remarked Moser-Marie.

"Oh, I remember that evening," replied Elise. "I think that was a very nice thing of him to do. He comes across as rough on the outside, and he is not a man of many words. So he picked some flowers, like you would say a word of thanks or write a thank-you note."

"All right." Moser-Marie nodded. There was relief in her voice. "I feel better knowing that you can cope with his antics. You are something like a miracle worker! Enough said, and this conversation will not go anywhere. I will probably see you tomorrow at the market."

"Have a good evening, Moser-Marie."

*T*he work was done for Elise. A vegetable stew was keeping warm on the stove. Mr. Ludwig was not home yet, and Elise sat down at the piano. As she did not want to pick through any music sheets, she started to play what came to mind. This time it was a perky, small sonata, which Beethoven had written. She did not know when it had been written. She just played it. There was a playful, little minuet that concluded the piece.

Mr. Ludwig had entered, but he did not make his presence known. He stood quietly, listening and reflecting. This was one of his early piano sonatas, still very much influenced by the old master Joseph Haydn, who had been his teacher at that time. It had not been the best time. He and Joseph Haydn simply had not seen eye to eye. He was trying to develop his own style of music, and old Haydn had shaken his head and warned him that this new style would not be easily accepted and people could find it confusing. He had switched teachers, as he found it too frustrating to deal with Papa Haydn's well-meaning but conservative attitude.

So this was a piece of music that he had put away over ten years ago, and he had not expected it to go anywhere. And here it was, being played with freshness and energy. He shook his head, thoroughly puzzled. How did Elise get ahold of this music? For a moment he wanted to shout and accuse Elise of riffling through his music sheets, but he caught himself. No, this was unfounded! The sonata was not even here in his belongings. It was in Vienna! He waited till she was finished playing.

"Bravo!" he said. "That was very well played. But you have me puzzled. I wrote that sonata over ten years ago and stashed it away. I don't remember whether I even took it to any of the publishers. Where did you get the music? Where did you learn it?"

Elise stood up from the bench, but he shook his head. "No, sit down. I just had to think! It would be nice if I could hear some more. But tell me first how you learned this piece."

Elise looked at him. "I'll tell you. I have a piano teacher at Meyer's music school. I have been taking lessons since my ninth birthday."

He was eager to know more. "Where is that? Are you from Vienna?"

"I am from Heiligenstadt, Mr. Ludwig. The music school is in Heiligenstadt."

He smiled. "Now you are joking! There is no music school in this village."

Elise hesitated, but at his encouraging nod, she continued. "You will call me disturbed or crazy, just like the others in the convent. But I am telling you the truth. I am from Heiligenstadt. A vehicle on the road hit me, and the nuns nursed me back to health. This all sounds perfectly normal, but in my reality, I live in the year 2002, even though everybody has told me that this is the year 1802. It is difficult for me to adapt to this change. The people's reality here is not my reality."

Mr. Ludwig looked at her. What she had said was unusual, but he had to think that there was a rational explanation. "To me you look perfectly normal. You are not a ghost. You are a young lady, and from what I have seen, you are too gifted to work as a housekeeper. One day you may be a very good musician. Personally, I believe that you had a bad injury to your head and that may have disturbed your thinking. But this does not make you a disturbed person."

He sighed and looked in the distance. "Sometimes my reality is not other people's reality either, so I can understand that it may be difficult for you to fit in. When I came to Vienna, I felt out of place in this big city, despite well-meaning friends and their help. I don't like the pomp and ceremony of courts. The nobility started their existence as infants in swaddling clothes, just like everybody else. That does not entitle them to feel superior. I refuse to bow before them! People are scandalized at this behavior, but, quite frankly, that is not my problem. Also, my music has been criticized by one of my teachers, Joseph Haydn, for being too difficult for people to understand. There are some dark moments when I feel misunderstood. It can feel like a very lonely journey. So I have been accused of being disrespectful, arrogant, and ill behaved."

After this statement Elise could not suppress a giggle. He grinned sheepishly. "Well, yes, granted, I can be ill behaved. You have a way of pointing things out in a very direct fashion!"

Elise took a deep breath. "I never thought that you would have these difficulties."

He sighed. His head was bowed down, and there was an expression of sadness, almost defeat, in his face. Slowly he stated, "Oh, yes, I do have my difficulties. I have been unwell, and so I came to Heiligenstadt for the summer to take the curative waters at the bathhouse. My doctor thought that all of this would help—the waters and living in the serene setting of the country.

Doctors—ha! They are not privileged to know everything either! I just spend another gulden for a few consultations." His voice sounded bitter. "If that's not enough, my hearing now is giving me more trouble than during the last year."

Elise listened breathlessly. It was like she was hearing a very private confession.

"The constant ringing and buzzing in my ears…it is almost intolerable at times," he said unhappily. "There are times when I feel like I am entering an abyss of despair. What will I do if my hearing fails me? I'm in a trade that relies on hearing more than a lot of other professions do. As a musician, I need to hear not only now but also in the future. Right now I feel like I am turning into a miserable, crippled, worthless man. Oh, the irony! Only the old are supposed to have these afflictions, but I'm only thirty-one years old!" He buried his face in his hands, and his shoulders shook.

Elise felt like she did the time when her friend Mark had failed an exam—a failure that would set him back in his studies. He had been devastated. She had quietly sat with him and stroked his hair and told him that this was not the end of the world. She could not offer Beethoven comfort like that. After all, he was her employer!

She sat down and cautiously touched his shoulder. "Mr. Ludwig, I can feel how upsetting this is. But, first of all, you cannot see only the gloom and doom of what may be or what may not be in the future. We simply cannot know what the future will hold; we have to live now, not in the past and not in the future! And I don't believe for one moment that people who lose their hearing are worthless cripples. Their lives have just taken a different turn than expected. My grandfather is almost deaf. Yes, it is hard for him. At times he feels left out, but we love him. And he is still the same person that loves us too. Your true friends will always love and value you as the person you are." With emphasis she continued. "Yes, you are a musician, but you have the music in you—in your mind, in your heart. I have seen you write your music scores without ever playing them on an instrument. This proves to me that you hear the music within yourself, without even relying on your ears."

He looked up, astonished and intrigued by her statement. "It is beyond me how you can know this, but there is truth in what you are saying." The dark clouds seemed to lift. He stretched and shrugged his shoulders. "You are right, Elise. We all have to live with our personal challenges, and it can be very trying and seem impossible at times. But let's not dwell on those difficulties further today! Can you play another piece of music?"

"One of yours?"

His eyes were animated. "Certainly, which one will it be?"

Elise leaned back. "It's the second movement of your *Grande Sonate Pathétique*. I love it, because it is everything: quiet, comforting, and later much more dynamic." She played, and time went on.

Evening was falling as she played. Mr. Ludwig picked up the candlesticks and lit the candles. The evening shadows softened the differences of time and place for Elise, and her listener sat with his eyes half closed and found solace in music, which let him forget his own difficulties. When she had finished playing the movement, he put his hand on her arm. "There was this part right in the beginning..." He sat down beside her and played some of the bars. "Here! This should be played in a ritardando. Just do it again, and just slow it down somewhat."

Elise understood. "Oh, I see what you mean." She repeated the passage.

"Yes, that's exactly what I had in mind," he replied. "I don't have the music sheets here, but I do remember this piece quite well. In the middle of the movement—right here!—you can use the pedal a bit more. It increases the dramatic mood."

Elise repeated the passage as she had been instructed. "Yes, I like it this way," he said. He was pleased with her progress. Elise looked up with a start. "What is it now?" he questioned.

"Oh, goodness! It's long past your suppertime. I had it all prepared, and the food is probably stone-cold by now!"

He laughed. "Don't worry about that. I'll eat it anyways."

Elise stood up and brought supper to the table. Thankfully the heavy cast-iron pot on the stove had held the heat, and the food was still edible. He did not seem to mind the delay.

"Tomorrow we will work some more on the *Pathétique*," he said. "You are not my piano student, but I would love to show you some more about the music."

Elise just beamed. "I feel so lucky that you are doing that! But I can't pay you for lessons. I don't have that much money."

"It does not matter to me. Besides you are doing work for me. But I want to see you succeed. You are so close to playing this piece absolutely perfect."

"Thank you so very much. You are so generous, and I really appreciate it."

"It really gives me satisfaction to see your progress. So, have a good night."

She wished him a good night and went up to her room. This was exciting! There was so much more she wanted to learn. She would ask him tomorrow.

⌇

*M*r. Ludwig kept his word. After the evening work had been done, he asked Elise to sit down at the piano. She played the same movement of the *Pathétique* again, and he was satisfied that she was able to reproduce the passages they had discussed the evening before. "You are a student that would make any teacher proud!" he acknowledged after she had finished playing. "Has your teacher ever suggested that you should give a concert?"

"Yes, and I also prepared a piece with another student that we were supposed to play, one of your sonatas for four hands."

"Show me!" he encouraged her.

"It goes like this…" Elise intoned the first few bars.

"Of course! Yes, a nice, little piece. I'm afraid that I don't have the music sheets here. But you seem to have a very good ability to memorize pieces. What do you play, the soprano or the bass section?"

"My friend played the bass. I played the soprano."

"Go ahead! It is still fresh in my mind and in my fingers too," he replied. She communicated the beginning to him, and they started. He did not interrupt till the first movement was done. "Not bad, but don't race away. It's lively, but not a presto. So a bit less speed…let's try this again, just a few bars."

Elise followed his instructions. They worked through all the sections of the first movement, after which he was pleased. "Good work, Elise! I thought that this summer I would not even think of teaching. But I'm changing my mind. It is very gratifying for me to work with you. Some students you can try to teach and nothing sticks, but you are a great student!" He paused for a moment and gave her a warm, encouraging smile. "I am thinking that you should be part of a concert in Vienna! Would you like working toward that? We can use the pieces that you are familiar with. Lady Lichnowsky and her husband love to give concerts in their salon."

Elise's head was spinning: this was like a dream, something she had never expected! She was learning so much more about the music pieces she had studied—and now a concert! Surprise was written in her face as she jumped up, threw her hands up in the air, and shouted an enthusiastic, "Yes! I'd love to do that! I'm so excited!"

He laughed good-naturedly. "Enough work for today! But I will send a note to the Lichnowskys, and then you and I can work on the pieces together."

*I*t was exciting for Elise to think of a concert and preparing music pieces for it. Luckily she had time to do it! Also it was surprising to her that Mr. Ludwig had come up with the idea.

She had to think back to the beginning of her time working for him. He had been such a cantankerous, difficult man, and the first days had been a rocky start, but somehow the episode of thunder and lightning was over. Moser-Marie had called her a miracle worker. But she could not quite see her neighbor's point. After all she was just doing her work and trying to do it well. It was still surprising to her that under this rough shell was a person that was thoughtful, patient and generous with his time teaching her. He was cordial, always encouraging her in her efforts, and whenever he criticized a passage, he did it in a gentle and constructive way. She could ask questions, and it was like she was talking to a person who treated her like a good friend and fellow-musician. It was an observation that amazed her.

One morning she went off to the market for the daily needs. It was a warm day, and everybody was out early, before the heat of this August day would be too intense. In the crowd of people she caught a glimpse of Mr. Ludwig. This was highly unusual. He had left to go to the mineral baths, or so he had stated. Maybe he had forgotten to mention a necessary purchase to her. She went about her errands, greeted her neighbors and went back to the house.

As she entered the kitchen she noticed a large bouquet of lavender on the kitchen table. It filled the room with a beautiful fragrance. A small, square paper-wrapped package lay beside it. Puzzled she looked at the flowers and the package. Where did that come from? Had Moser-Marie been here? She would sometimes leave a little something from her garden on the kitchen table. Elise stopped short, when she noticed a small note written on the package. No, this was not from her neighbor. It read

" For you, Elise. I hope that you'll enjoy the fragrance of summer during your work.

Yours Ludwig."

Elise felt a flutter in her stomach. He never said much, and he had never written a note to her either. Curiously she unwrapped the small package. It was a bar of lavender soap. What a beautiful scent! This man had a way to surprise and amaze her. She had to smile. So, that's why he had been visiting the market early this morning! She always enjoyed it, when he brought a bunch of summer flowers from his walks, but she never expected that he would surprise her with a small gift. There was no reason for it, no birthday, no special occasion. The gift moved her, and the fragrance of the flowers reminded her of him during her morning work.

The morning went by fast, and Mr. Ludwig arrived at his usual time. Elise stepped out of the kitchen. "Mr. Ludwig, this was a beautiful surprise! Thank you so much for the beautiful bouquet. And the soap has such a wonderful fragrance!"

There was warmth in his eyes and emotion in his voice. "Oh Elise, this is just a small token. I'm so glad that you like it." He seized her hands in his and looked at her with an intensity that made her heart pound and her head spin. "I cannot even start to describe how much you have come to mean to me, Elise."

She blushed to the roots of her hair and smiled at him. It was an effort for her to focus on her work. Yes, she had to admit it to herself that he had come to mean more and more to her as well. There was the powerful connection of the music that they worked on together. Also there were their personalities, both of them strong willed and outspoken. Here was her, searching for a place in a time that was unfamiliar to her. And there was him, seeking to be understood by others. Was it simply friendship that had developed between them?

If she was honest with herself, she had to admit that their connection was becoming more intense and more profound than friendship. There was the powerful pull of attraction to him. This feeling had become stronger, but she needed time to think. She was grateful to him that he had shown his affection for her in such a considerate and respectful way. He was restraining himself and did not want to overwhelm her, but she had read in his eyes that he wanted more than just friendship.

The dim light of a warm September evening filled the room, and a full moon rose in the sky. Elise's work was done, and Mr. Ludwig had gone out. She enjoyed the stillness of the evening and used her free time to work on the music pieces she had been studying under Mr. Ludwig's guidance. After a long time she was satisfied with her results. Her mind wandered back to her lessons with Mrs. Meyer. She looked through the window into the evening light, and her mind went back to the last piece she had practiced, the *Moonlight* Sonata.

Her fingers found the familiar melody and the intricate broken chords without difficulty. It seemed so long ago that she had last played the piece, but it came back immediately in her mind. She was as fascinated with the piece now as she had been when she'd played it before. However, as she continued playing it she was overwhelmed by the memories that were attached to it. There was the street that led to the music studio and the creaky stairs to the door. She still heard her mother's admonitions, but also Mrs. Meyer's encouraging words. There was Mark, clowning around before they played the sonata for four hands together, and his invitation to go out in the evening. She painfully remembered the feeling when her mother told her she did not want her to continue practicing the sonata, as it involved a bigger time commitment. Yes, it had been an end to a dream.

Then there was the accident that had turned her world upside down. Now she would definitely not be playing the *Moonlight* Sonata at the concert. She and Mark would not be playing the piece they had been practicing together. What was the reason for her being here? Tears ran down her cheeks as she felt the distress of living in a time that was so different from her life before.

And yet she had to think there must be a reason. She had not spent her time in vain, as she had encouraged two persons, Josepha and Sister Martha, to think and change the course of their lives. Now she was in the role of a humble housekeeper, but she was working in the home of a musician whose work she had studied, and she was learning much more from him. Deep down she knew that no matter what happened, there would always be a reason and a purpose in her life, even if they were not clearly visible or understandable to her at this point. These thoughts gave her comfort and hope.

It was late in the evening. Mr. Ludwig was on his way home after having spent a pleasant evening with some friends, which included Prince Lichnowsky and his wife. They had made a trip into the country and were staying at a nearby mansion. There had been a lively exchange of news, and the Lichnowskys were pleased to hear that his new housekeeper had been a good choice. Lady Lichnowsky was eager to see how his summer residence had been transformed into a pleasant home since her last visit. Spontaneously, Mr. Ludwig invited them for lunch the next day, and they were happy to accept the offer.

The small road in Heiligenstadt was quiet, but he was not surprised when he heard the sound of the piano coming from his residence. He stood still. Of course he recognized the melody, but he could not believe what he heard. This was his most recently composed work, the Sonata in C-sharp Minor *Quasi una Fantasia*—the piece that was like a fantasy. This was not even published! The music was not known to anybody except him. He walked faster. Either Elise had a pact with the devil, or she had the qualities of a clairvoyant. Inwardly he shook his head. Pact with the devil! Medieval superstition and nonsense! Swiftly but quietly he entered the house.

The piece was beautifully played, with emotion and gentleness, and it left him with a sense of awe and admiration. He had written it and imagined it, and she played it with such a sense of sentiment and understanding that it left him speechless. It was like the person playing it had taken a look into his mind and played the piece with an authenticity he had only imagined. How did she practice it to bring it so close to perfection?

He knew that it was fruitless to ask any questions, as he knew the answer already: she would explain that she had studied the music with her music teacher. And this was where his reality differed from the reality that was hers. There were things between heaven and earth that seemed to be humanly impossible, and yet they existed. Often people associated these supernatural events with something that was demonic, horrifying, and cursed. He could not relate to these sentiments. There was nothing demonic or horrifying about Elise or the way she played the piano. It was just something that went beyond anybody's imagination, including his own.

He stepped into the room and stood beside the piano. Elise acknowledged his presence with a nod and continued till she had finished the dreamy movement. He noticed that her face was serious. It looked like she had cried. She stood up from the instrument.

Mr. Ludwig intently looked at her. "Elise, I have never heard this piece played by anybody else before except me. You have played it exactly the way I imagined it. This is like a special gift you have given me, and I want to thank you from the bottom of my heart." He looked at her. "You are sad this evening, even though you are playing the piano, which always has been a source of joy for you. What is upsetting you so much?"

Her face showed a great effort to stay calm. "Yes, I have cried. You see, I have memories; there are memories of my music school when I studied this piece. And I had dreams that I would play it at a concert. I tried so hard. But then my mother was worried that my schoolwork would suffer, and she told my teacher that I should not practice it further, as it would be too much. And on the way home, a vehicle on the road hit me. I did not pay attention when I crossed the road."

He sat down on the piano bench beside her. The information was somewhat overwhelming for him, as she clearly still believed that she lived in a world two hundred years later. But in her face was the timeless expression of human suffering. He saw a person who had to abandon a treasured dream, and it touched his heart. *There has to be a solution,* he thought as he looked at her. "Elise, I cannot help you live in any other time than this one. But if it comforts you, I want you to follow your dream and see it come to fulfillment. I can teach you all you need to know about presenting this sonata. Would you like to play it at a concert in Vienna at a later date?"

Her previously sad face brightened. "I can never thank you enough!"

"It is late," he said, "and tomorrow I'll have some company at the noon hour. It is time to get some rest."

"Yes, I know, but there is one thing I wanted to ask you, Mr. Ludwig. Could you please play this movement one more time? I mean, it would be the best thing that could happen to me, if I could really hear it the way you were thinking it should be played."

He looked into eyes that pleaded with him, and he wanted her to feel better and be at peace. "If it makes you happy, I will gladly do it." He gave her a warm smile, sat closer to the instrument, and started playing as she watched his agile fingers and listened, spellbound. He looked up after he finished and saw her face, no longer distressed and sad but relaxed and happy. He sighed. "Some evenings should never come to an end," he began, but he caught himself. "But there is tomorrow. I am expecting the Lichnowskys. You remember Lady Lichnowsky, who came to the convent and brought you here? She will come with her husband at the noon hour."

Elise stood up and turned to go. "Thanks for everything you showed me today, and good night, Mr. Ludwig. I'll be up early, and you can tell me about any special wishes for your company." She flew up the stairs. Sleep came easy, and the music she had heard seemed to permeate all her dreams.

⌒

*I*t had been a busy morning for Elise. She had gone to the market early to buy all the necessary items for lunch with the Lichnowskys. It was not particularly difficult, but she wanted everything to be perfect. Critically, she looked around the rooms to be sure that everything looked tidy and comfortable for the guests. Mr. Ludwig had gone out, as usual.

Elise needed to make one more run to get water, and she ran into her neighbor. "Good morning, Moser-Marie!" she called.

The older woman eyed her with friendly interest. "You are a busy girl this morning, Elise! Don't work too hard."

"It is just busier today, as Mr. Ludwig is having company for lunch."

The neighbor looked surprised. "Company? Well, that's the first time I ever saw him invite anybody. He is such a solitary person! This should be good for him! Everybody needs friends and good company."

"I just hope that I'm doing everything right," remarked Elise.

Moser-Marie gave her an encouraging pat on the shoulder. "Girl, you have nothing to worry about. You have done so much work here and turned a stable into a beautiful home. And this has been good for Mr. Ludwig. He has changed from his withdrawn attitude and always says hello to the neighbors. What is more, there is no yelling, no shouting, and everything is quiet and peaceful. Before you arrived it was never quiet, let alone peaceful! You will do just fine, Elise! Just smile! Do you know that you have such a pretty smile?"

"Oh, Moser-Marie! Thanks for encouraging me."

"If you need some flowers on the table, just go into my backyard. There are some beautiful fall asters and sunflowers. Go and help yourself!"

"Good idea! You are an angel! Thank you, Moser-Marie!" Elise hurried back and went out into the small backyard of her neighbor. Sunflowers were blooming, a golden profusion that matched the golden shade of the high-noon sunlight. Purple asters created lively color spots in a corner of the garden. Elise picked a few stems and went inside to arrange them in a glass jug. Above the front door of the house, an arbor of vines was spreading out. The dark-blue and golden-green grapes would be beautiful on a plate on the table.

Elise went up to her room and found a clean apron. Critically she looked into the small mirror on the wall and quickly twisted her hair into a nice style. Her thoughts went back to the time when Josepha had first taught her how to put her hair up. It seemed so long ago. Josepha, Sister Martha...where were they now, and how were they doing? She stopped herself. There was no time to get lost in thoughts. She had to be ready to look after the guests.

There were voices outside. Mr. Ludwig and his friends were at the door, and she quickly went about completing the last finishing touches for lunch. They were having a quiet conversation, and she waited. Mr. Ludwig called for her, and she entered the room. They had taken their places at the table, and Elise greeted them.

Lady Lichnowsky approvingly looked at her. "Well, Elise, how nice to see you here," she exclaimed. "I am so pleased that you are looking after our friend's household."

Mr. Ludwig added, "I didn't mention it earlier: without her work, my dear friends, I would have never dared to invite you to my home for lunch."

The Lichnowskys laughed good-naturedly at this statement, as they knew only too well about their friend's disorganized lifestyle. Elise served them their lunch and quietly went back into the kitchen. It was time to take a break. The guests sat in the living area, immersed in a lively conversation.

Nine

MAGICAL DAYS

*E*lise went outside and sat on the bench to read a book she'd found. It was a volume of poems by the poet Johann Wolfgang von Goethe. She knew some of them from school, but she also knew from school that these two geniuses would only meet about ten years later. She found it interesting that Mr. Ludwig was also interested in reading poetry, as everything in his life was centered around music.

Elise enjoyed the quietness of the early afternoon hour. It was one of those glorious sun-filled September days. A shadow fell on the pages. It was Lady Lichnowsky, joining her outside.

"I am glad to see that you are taking a moment of leisure," the countess said.

Elise cautiously looked up from her reading. Was that a reprimand?

The countess's lively eyes glanced at the book. "What have you found to read except music in this household?"

"It's a book of poems by the poet Johann Wolfgang von Goethe," Elise answered. "There are some very beautiful ones—have you read them?"

"Yes, I have! It's good that you are taking an interest in literature too. You seem to be a young lady of many talents."

This was almost too much of a compliment. "I like many things, but music is my favorite," Elise replied.

"I know that; our friend has told us about that too, and I wanted to extend a very cordial invitation to you to visit us in Vienna. Our friend mentioned that he would arrange a concert program for a group of our friends and our family."

Elise was pleasantly surprised. "Thank you very much. I gladly accept your invitation, Lady Lichnowsky."

The lady continued. "Elise, I do not want to criticize you, but you will need some clothes that are more fitting for the big city."

Elise's smile was labored. She would go and ask Moser-Marie whether there was a place where she could get an inexpensive dress. Or maybe she could find something suitable at the market.

"It's still the same as before, Lady Lichnowsky," Elise explained. "I do not own anything else. Mr. Ludwig is paying me, but I am saving my money. So it has never occurred to me, so far, that I might need better clothes. But I understand what you mean. Here I am in the country, and Vienna is different, of course. I'll see what I can do about that."

Lady Lichnowsky shook her head. "No, no, my dear Elise! That is not what I am suggesting at all. One of my daughters is of similar stature as you. You are saving your money! This is very laudable! When you come to Vienna, you can try some of her dresses, and my seamstress will do any necessary adjustments. I certainly don't want to hurt your feelings, but you simply deserve better. So, do not worry about a thing. I look forward to seeing you in Vienna at our salon—as a musician and not as a housekeeper." It pained her to see a gifted young girl living her life without the chance of getting more suitable employment and moving up in the world. In a way she thought that Elise was never meant to scrub floors, carry water, and do kitchen work. She did all her work exceedingly well, but it did not seem to be the work she was destined to do.

Even though Lady Lichnowsky did not know anything about the girl's background, she felt that Elise was living in circumstances that did not fit her at all. Her friend Ludwig had a rare jewel in her; she was a very pretty young lady, musical, intelligent, industrious, and, if he had any sense, he should look at her as a young woman he could marry one day. But, of course, she was still very young, and she had not been here for long. Lady Lichnowsky looked at the young girl's face, and her happiness and excitement was obvious. "We'll see you in Vienna not too long from now, Elise!"

After they parted, Elise went about her work as usual, but there was an undercurrent of anticipation and excitement. She would go to Vienna! Of course she knew this big, vibrant city, but this would be an adventure. This would not be the Vienna she remembered—the Vienna with lots of cars and buses, glitzy stores, and street-side cafes. It would be very different. All the landmarks, all the old buildings, she would probably recognize, and Saint Stephen's towers would be standing as proud and tall as she knew them, but there would be lots of items she would not know at all.

~~~

*M*r. Ludwig followed a predictable schedule. He would go to the bathhouse in Heiligenstadt either in the morning or in the afternoon. Frequently he went for his solitary walks. As before, he was not a man of many words, but often he brought a bouquet of flowers he had gathered on his walks and handed them to Elise with a smile. His usually serious face had softened. Nothing had changed about his morning routines, and he would appear at one for his lunch, but there were no outbursts and no quarrelsome remarks. He never failed to give her a warm smile and a heartfelt thank-you after she had served him his meals and at the end of the day when her work was done.

As time went on, he seemed to be more at ease and smiled more often. Elise thought that his summer in the relaxed ambience of the country village had contributed to his well-being, and she found it pleasant to work for somebody who was friendly and appreciative of her work. He was not exactly an example of orderliness. She still found shirts and jackets draped over armchairs or tables, but things were definitely more civilized: he did not leave mud-covered boots in the closet. Also he seemed to enjoy that his place had been turned into a relaxing and comfortable residence, and this had a positive impact on his more relaxed mood and his well-being.

There were hours though, where he seemed to be preoccupied and in a dark mood. Once Elise had asked him whether his day had been unpleasant or difficult. She saw the pained expression on his face, and he had freely shared that he was concerned about his hearing. The doctors had not found an answer for him, and the curative waters of Heiligenstadt had not been as helpful as he had hoped they would be. Elise had agreed that this was disappointing for him but also pointed out that a summer's rest away from a lot of pressure would have a beneficial effect on anybody who had been in need of a break from the daily demands.

In the evenings, however, he was an entirely different person. He seemed to come out of his solitary existence and was talkative and excited. In the meantime, he had prepared a program for the musical evening in Vienna, and after he had finished any composition work, they would sit down together and practice the pieces that Elise would present. She had practiced the *Grande Sonate Pathétique*, and they were working on the final touches of the Sonata in C-sharp Minor. Mr. Ludwig grew animated: this was the piece that had not been published yet, and he was fascinated by the prospect that this would be its first performance ever.

One evening, when the moonlight shone through the windows, Elise looked up after she had finished the piece. "You know, this piece has the perfect name, *Moonlight* Sonata. The first movement sounds like the mood of a moonlit evening. You can imagine moonlight on quiet water!"

He smiled. "You have a lot of fantasy, Elise. You surprise me."

Elise elected not to tell him that she only knew it by this name. It was again one of the points where the year 1802, into which she had been thrown, collided with the year 2002, from which she had come.

They had treated all the concert pieces like jewels: the pieces had been polished to a flawless shimmer, and Elise had practiced them under his tutelage. He was an exacting but surprisingly patient teacher. Small mistakes did not bother him, and he encouraged her to go with the flow of the music and convey the feelings it was meant to express. Also, he was confident that the concert would be a success.

Mr. Ludwig had gone out for the morning, and it was close to the time he would come to the house for his lunch. Elise had finished her morning work, when there was the whinnying of a horse outside. She looked out and saw a rider. He had tied the horse to a post on the roadside.

There was a loud knock on the door.

She opened and saw a young man with a satchel over his shoulder. "Are you looking for anybody?"

The man gave her an ingratiating smile. "I'm a courier for the count of Waldstein in Vienna, and I bring a letter for Mr. Ludwig van Beethoven. The count would like a reply, and I can wait for it to take the message back to Vienna."

Elise saw a face that was a bit too smooth, too arrogant, and she saw eyes that had the look of a predator. She felt immediately uncomfortable. "I am sorry, but Mr. Ludwig is not home at the moment. He should not be long."

The man took a step into the house. He gave Elise a smile. "This is no problem. I will wait for him. In the meantime I am delighted to have your charming company."

Elise gave him an even look. This man had stepped into the house without even being invited in. She found it difficult to stay calm and polite. "I think it would be better, if you could wait outside. I'm busy here, and you will meet Mr. Ludwig right there."

His smile became impertinent. "After this long ride it would be a pleasure to enjoy the company of a beautiful lady. It is kind of lonely outside, and from all appearances you are alone too. How perfect can it get?" He took a step towards her.

Elise stepped back. "I don't remember that I invited you to come into the house. Would you please leave? I'm perfectly fine without your company!" With disgust she noticed that the man reeked of alcohol. His stare and smile unnerved her.

She could run out the back door. Too late! He had grabbed her arm and wanted to pull her closer. "Leave me alone! Get out of the house!' She yelled at the top of her voice, and with her free hand she hit the man square in his face, when the front door flew open and Mr. Ludwig entered. "What is going on here?"

The man immediately stepped away from Elise. "I'm here as a courier from the count of Waldstein. I was just offering the young lady my company, and I'm waiting for your reply to his letter."

Ludwig saw the terror in Elise's eyes. Coldly he looked at the man. His voice was ominously quiet. "As it is obvious from the appearance of your face your generous offer has not been too well received by the lady." He pointedly looked at the red mark on the man's cheek that Elise's hand had left. There was an almost murderous glint in Mr. Ludwig's eyes, and his voice rose to a shout. "If you value your life I would recommend that you leave this second. And if you think that you can honor this lady with your questionable company, I can assure you that she is in better company than yours. Get out of this house! You can wait for the reply out there. It will just take me a minute." He pointed to the door.

The self-assured arrogance had vanished from the face of the courier and had been replaced by a look of fear. Without a word he bolted out the door. Mr. Ludwig took a deep breath. There was outrage in his face, as he looked at Elise. "Has he hurt you? Are you all right?" He took a step towards her and put his arms protectively around her.

Elise nodded." This was scary." She felt unsteady on her legs and held on to him. He saw that she was still shaking, and put his hand comfortingly on her shoulder. "Sit down for a bit. I have to quickly write this note, so this chap can get on his way." Quickly he penned a note, folded it, and went outside.

He returned and sat down beside her. He had never seen her unnerved and upset like that before.

"If I had only come home earlier, then all of this would not have happened." His arm was wrapped around her, and she leaned her head against his shoulder. He gave her a soft kiss on her cheek. "I just want you to feel better, Elise."

She smiled at him and kissed him back. "Thank you for your company. It means a lot to me."

He looked at her, and Elise saw more in his intense look than just concern for her and fierce protectiveness. There was an expression of deep affection and the undercurrent of a question whether she returned his affection.

She leaned against his shoulder, and he saw her answer clearly in her face. She did not hide her affection to him. "I am so glad that you are here."

He nodded solemnly and kept her in his arm in a gesture that was both, comforting and loving.

After the noonday meal he stood up and looked through some papers on his desk.

He found a stack of music sheets and put them together. "The courier sent a note that the count of Waldstein wanted to discuss some music pieces with me tomorrow. It looks like he will be commissioning some work. So I will have to go to Vienna tomorrow for the day."

Elise nodded." I see. You probably will have to leave early enough."

He grimaced. Getting up early was not something he liked. "Yes, there is the coach that leaves at six in the morning, and I guess that I will have to take that one. I really had no plan to go on an extra trip to Vienna, but this is about business. I'll be back in the evening, whenever the last coach is leaving. It should be before it is getting night."

He looked at her with concern in his face. "After this unsavory visitor today I'm concerned about you. Maybe keep the doors locked when you are alone here. I know that you can put up a good fight, but I want you to be safe and not bothered by some sober or drunk idiot."

Elise agreed." I'm not afraid, but yes, I'll be careful."

She started her day earlier, so Mr. Ludwig could leave in time. After that the day was quieter than usual. She had her work, but there was a void at the noon hour. Mr. Ludwig did not come back for lunch.

She felt a short sting of sadness, as she noticed that she missed him. This feeling was new to her, and it amazed her. She had felt the deepening connection between him and her earlier, but she had never fully admitted it to herself.

In the afternoon she went for a quick walk out to the field and collected a large bunch of field flowers. She wanted to share some with her neighbor. A large bouquet was for the dining table, but she also put a small bouquet on his bedside table. She had never done this before, and it had been a spontaneous idea. Somehow she was surprised about herself.

Why did she do it? This was not just the idea of making a home more livable. If she was really honest, she had to admit that she cared for him.

In the stillness of the warm fall afternoon she went outside into the little backyard. She cut off wilted flowers and picked weeds.

In this serene little yard she had the time to listen within herself. She came from a different time and was about to fall in love with a man of a different era.

At first glance this seemed impossible. And yet, what was time? She looked around. Outside in the garden a sense of timelessness prevailed. The bench, the tree, the garden, the twittering birds could fit into any time. It looked the same in any century, whether it was the year 1802 in which she was now living or whether it would be in 2002.

Time could be something utterly relative, and a century seemed only like a grain of sand in the large hourglass of time. Sometimes she found it easier to overlook all the differences. She looked at her dress. Yes, it was different, but this did not bother her any more. People around her had the same concerns living their lives and had the same emotions. Some were good people, but she also met unpleasant persons. The human experience was the same for all of them, the joys as well as the troubles, no matter in which century they lived.

There were the neighbors in the village that accepted her as one of theirs without any questions. They never treated her like an outcast or a foreign body. It was her who had the feeling that she was a foreign body. She could not deny who she was. There was still the ache of having been transplanted.

She was cut off from the people that were dear to her. It hurt. Would it ever stop hurting? This she did not know, but she had to grow into this new environment, and she experienced growing pains.

Also there was the realization that life went on relentlessly, and she could choose to either feel like a prisoner of her fate or she could choose to not feel like a helpless victim. It was up to her to see the gift of living every day, no matter what circumstances surrounded her.

She could not see Mark and could not be close to him. There was no mother she could confide in. This time was not accessible to her, and she accepted that she had to allow herself to rebuild her life. By the same token it was a process that took time and effort.

She could not live in the yesterday or tomorrow. She had to live now. It was useless to ask why her life had been redirected. In time she would know the answer, and for now she was responsible to infuse her life with meaning.

The gardening was done, and she went back into the house in deep thought. Moser-Marie had left a bowl with plums on the kitchen table. This was so nice of her good neighbor! She would go over later, thank her, and bring her the flowers too. She went to the washbowl and took the bar of lavender soap-Ludwig's surprise gift- to wash her hands after the garden work.

There were people who were kind and loving, and she accepted that they had become part of her life now.

Her glance went into the living room. There was the piano and the music sheets, and it was music, which connected her so much with Ludwig. Everything in the room had become a source of familiar comfort to her. There were Ludwig's boots under a chair and a jacket draped over the backrest. She caught herself wishing that he would be back soon. With a sense of wonder she noticed that she could allow his affection into her life. She could see the common ground they both had, and she also treasured the closeness of their relationship.

There was love, a timeless emotion, which was defying a gap of centuries. It had to grow like a tender plant. He had shown to her that he was willing to nurture it, and in her heart she knew that she wanted to do the same.

She was grateful for this afternoon of stillness and reflection. The time to think had cleared her mind.

Quickly she paid her neighbor a visit and brought her the bouquet of flowers. After that she prepared some supper, as she knew that Mr. Ludwig would come back after a long day in Vienna. She did not feel like sitting down and eating; she would wait for him.

Elise heard the church bell that tolled seven times. Her work was done. She should feel relaxed, but there was an undercurrent of restlessness in her. She had to smile at herself, as she was as nervous as a girl that was about to go on her first date, even though she did not have a date, but she was looking forward to Mr. Ludwig coming home. Evening sun turned into dusk, and she lit an oil lamp and put it on the windowsill by the front door. Curiously she opened a window and listened into the stillness of the evening. A group of people was talking and laughing in the distance, and she heard the distant noise of wheels on the cobblestone street. It must be a coach that had arrived.

Steps were approaching the house. Mr. Ludwig entered. He looked tired, but his face brightened, when he saw Elise. She lit some candles and put supper on the table. They consumed their evening meal in silence.

He was more relaxed and leaned back in his chair. "It is good to be back, and I have a confession to make. I have missed you, Elise."

Her heart skipped a beat, and he saw an expression of happiness in her face, as she looked at him." You know, I worked in the morning and tried not to think much about you being away. But I missed you already at noon, and I'm so glad that you are home."

He stood up from the table and went to his bedroom. When he came back he looked at Elise, and his dark eyes were dancing. He held a small package in his hand. "Somebody by the name of Elise left flowers on my bedside table! What is the occasion?"

He saw her struggle for words for a moment, but then she found her voice. "Somebody who is very dear to me just returned from a day trip. Welcome back." Tenderly he took her hands into his and kissed her on both cheeks.

"My dear Elise, I had to think of you all day, and I wanted to bring you something from Vienna."

Elise unwrapped the small package and gasped. It was an exquisitely worked lace band for her hair and matching lace gloves. Her smile was radiant. "This is absolutely stunning! I have seen women wear these, but I never had beautiful lace like that. Thank you so very much! But you spent way too much money on me."

She was overwhelmed. Spontaneously she gave him a hug. He laughed out happily and held her hands." Oh Elise, you deserve so much more. And don't worry about the money! Going to Vienna was well worth the effort. The count of Waldstein gave me a big commission."

Elise tried on the gloves that fit perfectly. Her face was puzzled. "How could you know that they would fit me so well?"

He laughed into her eyes. "That was very easy. Each and every evening I sit at the piano and watch you play. By now I should know every detail of your hands."

Gently he held her hands and his heart leaped, when she looked at him with her open and adoring smile. "Mr. Ludwig, you are just incredible, and you will never stop to amaze me!"

⟜⟶

On the evening before they left for Vienna, she stayed at the instrument a bit longer. "I hope that you do not mind if I play a bit more?"

He was at his desk, writing out a music score. "No, I am working, but it does not bother me if you play."

Elise played whatever came to her mind. One was a small Schubert impromptu. He stopped for a moment and looked up with interest. "This is not something I have heard, but it's fun to listen to. Keep on improvising!"

Something came to Elise's mind: there was this little Beethoven piece that was called *Für Elise*. Well, it was her name, Elise! Why not intone it? She played a few bars.

Mr. Ludwig walked over from his desk. There was excitement in his tone as he said, "Stop for a moment! This is something that should be on paper!" He sat down beside her. "Let me continue for a bit. I think this is the way it should go on." He played another dozen bars.

Elise's eyes sparkled. "Yes, great! Now it's my turn!"

His face was puzzled for a moment, but then it broke into a happy smile, and he gave her a nod to carry on. Elise continued for a minute before he patted her on the shoulder and laughed. "You know, this is fun!" he said. "Here, let me go on for a bit." He continued the piece. It was like a game of throwing a ball between them.

Elise was excited. "This is not finished yet!" she exclaimed. "Please let me have a turn!" Elise continued into what was known to her as the middle section of the piece.

He did not interrupt her for some time, but he looked at her expectantly. "What about me? I think I'll carry on from here." Elise let him take over, and he ended the piece on a quiet, thoughtful note. He put his arm around her shoulders. "My dear Elise! This evening will be forever etched in my memory. There is something that I cannot understand, but I have to simply accept it: you are a person who is able to look into my soul. You took music that was just developing in my mind and in my thoughts, and you played it! This is so wonderful, so incredible, and I feel very grateful to you. You are a very special person to me."

Elise smiled at him. "You do not seem to know how special you are!"

He held his breath, and then very gently, he seized her hands and kissed them. "Are we soul mates, Elise? It feels like I have fallen in love with you."

There was a glow of happiness in her face, but she obviously had to think about his words. "I have always loved your music, Mr. Ludwig. I'm very young, and love is something that can grow."

He smiled at her. "You can call me just by my first name—Ludwig. My dear girl, you have a great deal of insight. And I too believe that love is something precious that has to grow." He gave her an affectionate hug. "I have an idea. Let's try to put this piece together right now, while it is fresh in our memories. This is our piece! I will name it after you. You start playing, and I'll start writing!"

Elise hugged him. "Thank you so much, my dear Ludwig! I'll treasure it as a very great gift from you." Together they played their piece once again. Every once in a while, Ludwig would concentrate on writing. The pen flew over the music sheet as he wrote down the melody. The bass accompaniment followed in quick succession, and the work grew with amazing speed. He was entirely focused on bringing their ideas to paper. It was long past midnight when he finished. He took a deep breath. They looked at each other and laughed. There was a sense of victory and happiness with the accomplishment they had achieved together.

"What an incredible evening! We made a piece of music together!" he marveled, and they sank into each other's arms in a comforting embrace. Time ticked by as he held her close, and she felt sheltered in his arms. "Oh, my dearest girl," he finally said, "it almost hurts to say good night! But it has to be… we are taking the coach to Vienna in the morning."

"Good night, my dear Ludwig, and thank you for all you have done," she whispered, kissing him on his cheek.

He gave her a long and intense look. His eyes were even darker, filled with restrained passion. He held her hands and kissed her back. "Good night, my dearest Elise!"

Quickly she went up to her room. Pictures whirled through her head. Everything was so confusing: she saw the warm smile on the face that had become softer and gentler than before; she remembered the agile fingers spinning melodies and the swift movement of his hand putting it all onto paper. This was Mr. Ludwig—Ludwig, as she was calling him now. But there was also the uncanny similarity to Mark, or Mr. B., as she called him because he did look so much like Ludwig. The pictures overlapped. She was longing for Mark's arms, yearning to be comforted in his embrace, to be understood and loved. Now she and Ludwig had shared an embrace between friends. This felt like a small spark that had turned into a gentle, warming flame. But she also knew that this flame was ready to take off into a roaring blaze next. There had been passion in his eyes, and she herself had felt the same emotion.

Who was it she was in love with? She knew that she was deeply in love with Mark, but that had been in 2002. Now she found herself in 1802. Was it Mark or was it Ludwig she loved—or could it be both? She was too tired to untangle this puzzling web. Somehow she had to live with both realities. Next she would be immersed into the world of Vienna in 1802. She fell into a fitful sleep. It was not simply the impending trip, but rather the evening before that was woven into her dreams. She dreamed of Ludwig and her creating the music piece, which he wanted to name after her. She still felt the warmth of his embrace. It was an exhilarating feeling that sent her flying high and made her want to be close to him. It was dawn when she woke up. She was restless and could not go back to sleep. Instead she decided to get ready and dressed for the trip. Carefully she tied the lace hair band –Ludwig's gift- into her hair. The coach would be leaving early, and she had to get the day started. For a moment she tried to make herself believe that the flutter in her stomach was just due to her being excited about the Vienna trip. No, she had to be honest with herself; she had to admit that this was not the full truth. More than anything she felt drawn to Ludwig, wanted to be in his presence, and her heart was beating faster, as she went downstairs. She entered the living area and was surprised to find him awake. He was writing music at his desk. He walked towards her, and stopped. "Elise, my dearest." He stretched out his arms, and she caught his gaze that showed his yearning for her. She felt the same almost painful longing for him that she had felt the night before, and it was the most natural feeling for her to come into his embrace.

He took a deep breath. "When I recently went to Vienna for the day I missed you all day. I also missed you last night. Forgive me for being so direct."

Elise gave him a long look. "Ludwig, this is entirely forgivable. I did not get much sleep either. It's not about me being excited to go on a trip. I just missed you too much."

Their embrace became passionate, and his mouth searched for hers. She felt his body pressed against her, an intoxicating sensation that blotted out any other thought.

He heaved a sigh of frustration. "I wish the coach would not leave so early this morning, but we really have to go now."

Reluctantly they stepped away from each other. Elise picked up her travel bag. "We won't miss each other all day, Ludwig. We are going to Vienna together." She was astonished at her own boldness, when she added, "I hope that we won't miss each other next night."

Her honest statement made him laugh out with happiness. He lifted her into his arms and kissed her her fervently. " Oh my love, I'll make sure we won't miss each other!"

⌒

uickly they left the house just in time to see the coach arrive, and they took their seats.

The carriage made its rumbling way toward the big city. Elise and Ludwig had started their journey in Heiligenstadt, and there were four other people sharing the ride. There was an older gentleman, who dozed comfortably in the upholstered seat and only opened his eyes and cursed whenever the vehicle hit an uneven stretch of road. Next to him was his wife, whose beady eyes darted back and forth between Ludwig and Elise with unconcealed curiosity. There were also two French-speaking ladies, all dressed up for a trip to the big city, incessantly chattering about their plans for their visit.

It took a full hour before they saw the church spires of the big city. Elise craned her neck to see familiar buildings. Yes, there were some structures she recognized!

Ludwig smiled at her. "I know, there is so much to see. It's a vibrant and exciting city. And now it feels even noisier than before, after being out in the country for a few months."

The lady who had observed both with vivid interest finally could not contain her curiosity any longer. "Somehow I think I know your face. Aren't you a musician from Vienna?"

Ludwig leaned back. "Well, there are so many famous musicians in this city of music," he commented. "I am just one of them."

She was not satisfied. "Aren't you Mr. Beethoven?"

"Yes, that's me," he replied.

"What about the young lady?"

The woman seemed to burst with curiosity, and Ludwig's facial expression showed that the constant questioning was starting to annoy him. Elise gave him a slight nudge. She gave the curious woman a square look. "Frankly, I am surprised this should be any of your concern, madame."

The woman's face showed surprise and embarrassment. After that interchange silence reigned in the coach, only interrupted by the steady clip-clop of the horses' hooves.

They arrived at their destination, and Ludwig got up and picked up their travel bags. He nodded shortly to the inquisitive cotraveler. "The young lady is quite right. Even a musician from Vienna is entitled to his privacy. Good afternoon."

They descended from the coach and walked down the road. Ludwig was amused. "You are certainly never at a loss for words that hit like arrows. And your nudge was a good signal." He smiled at her. "Oh, Elise! Every day with you is a surprise—a wonderful surprise!"

They arrived at a stately mansion in the middle of the city, and Ludwig pulled the doorbell. A servant appeared, greeted them, and ushered them into the drawing room. Both Lichnowskys were engaged in a game of chess but immediately got up. "Welcome back to Vienna, Ludwig—oh, and here is Elise too—how very nice! Sit down; be comfortable!"

Elise felt like she was visiting a museum, taking in the ornate furnishings and chandeliers with wax candles. Yes, it was a picture out of a different time. But it felt like a very comfortable, warm, and beautiful home. A servant entered and offered them coffee and some confections. Elise cautiously eyed the offerings. They looked unfamiliar, but she courageously took a bite and found that it was quite delicious.

The Lichnowskys asked one of their staff to show them to their rooms. Elise stared at the bedroom: it had ornate brocade curtains, plush carpets that muffled any sound, and a big, comfortable bed with a pile of pillows to sink into. She thought of her Spartan bedstead with its straw mattress under the roof and smiled. There was a water pitcher and a bowl for washing. She giggled when she spotted a chamber pot under the bed. *Different times, Elise*, she reminded herself. This room was luxury!

There was a knock at her door. Ludwig stood outside. "This is a bit more elaborate than my plain country residence," he remarked. "By the way, Lady Lichnowsky wanted to see you. She said something about a dress, and also they are offering to take us with their chaise to the Prater afterward. It's a nice afternoon!"

Elise remembered her previous conversation with the countess. "Yes, she had mentioned that she wanted to give me a dress to wear that is suitable for the big city. That's very generous of her."

He measured her with an admiring glance. "You always look very presentable, even in your country-style attire, Elise. You are beautiful."

She blushed and searched his face. He laughed and said, "Go and see her, and enjoy the dress. I'm not one who is an example of elaborate tastes."

Elise laughed as well. "You are absolutely wrong. It does not matter that you are not making a big fuss about the clothes you are wearing. But when it comes to having elaborate tastes, there are not many people who can beat you when it comes to music, Ludwig."

She went outside, and the countess took her to a small room. Several dresses were spread out on a sewing table. A seamstress was sitting at a worktable nearby, stitching the seams of a shirt. Lady Lichnowsky motioned for Elise to come and take a closer look. "These are the dresses that I thought would suit you best," she said, "and hopefully you'll feel comfortable in them. Let's see how they fit."

Elise stripped off her ordinary dress and put on a creation of white silk that was fitted around her bust and loosely flowed to her ankles. It looked like a Greek-style gown, which seemed to be the fashion of the day. The countess asked the seamstress to come over. With a few deft movements, the seamstress pinned it to fit Elise's figure.

"Try the other ones too," the countess encouraged Elise. "This one with the lace and pearls around the neckline is beautiful."

Elise slipped into a gown that looked like it was made for festive occasions. "Yes," said the countess, "and here is the one you should wear for the concert. What do you think?"

Incredulously, Elise looked at her image in the mirror. She saw herself entirely transformed from a very simple, country housemaid to a young lady that was fit to be seen in the high society of Vienna. She felt slightly overwhelmed. "I can't just take away your daughters' clothes," she protested.

"Oh, nonsense! These girls have enough! They don't even know how many outfits they have! Yes, I admit it; these young ladies are a bit spoiled. No, these are going to be your dresses. The seamstress is fixing a few stitches on the first one, so you can wear it right away. You are coming to the Prater with us, aren't you? No, I don't want any big thank-yous! I'm more than happy that you found some decent dresses!"

Elise's face was one big smile. "You are incredibly generous, Lady Lichnowsky!" Spontaneously she gave Lady Lichnowsky a hug.

The countess laughed heartily. "And you are one of the most refreshingly honest young girls I have ever met. It looks like the seamstress is finished, and you can wear your dress."

Elise slipped into the gown, and the countess looked pleased with the result. "Very nice! This looks like it was made for you, Elise. So, let's go to the Prater; come along!"

She and Elise stepped out of the house, where a chaise was waiting. Ludwig and his friend Prince Lichnowsky were standing outside, waiting for them. There was a benevolent glance from Ludwig's friend when he saw Elise in her new attire. What Elise saw in Ludwig's eyes was an expression of admiration and happiness. He offered her his arm as she climbed into the chaise, and he kept his arm around her a bit longer than necessary as they sat close together, opposite from Ludwig's friends.

After a short while they reached the Prater. It was a pleasant green space, and many Vienna residents were out walking and enjoying the beautiful afternoon hour. They went to one of the coffeehouses, where a string quartet was playing to entertain the listening crowd.

Of course, this was the Prater in 1802…there was no noise, no rides, no Ferris wheel, no trinket stands, and yet Elise noticed that the people enjoyed themselves. Like the others, she sat down on one of the wooden benches and listened to the music. Ludwig's hand was searching for hers, and she cast him a quick, furtive smile as their fingers entwined. There was unspoken closeness and happiness between both of them.

After the musicians finished playing, they went for a walk through the park area. They talked about the concert that would take place on the next evening. "We should have a bit of a practice this evening," Ludwig suggested. "It will help us to get a feel for the piano that we are going to use. Each instrument is different."

Lady Lichnowsky wondered, "Could we listen in, or are we too curious?"

"Of course! Feel free to listen. But at the same time, it is not like a concert. It is going to be work: we'll interrupt, we'll repeat, we'll talk about the passages and the dynamics. You may feel bored. By all means, join us to listen, but I will not be offended if you should want to leave."

They returned back to the home of the Lichnowskys, and dinner was served in the spacious dining room. Afterward Ludwig got up.

"Yes, I know, you will be anxious to practice a bit for the concert tomorrow," remarked Lady Lichnowsky. "Let's go over to the salon." She opened a set of wide doors, and they entered a large hall that was reserved for balls, concerts, and other entertainment. It was a beautiful room, with elaborate wall murals and large windows. Several chandeliers hung from the ceiling. For this evening, they only lit a chandelier that was close to the grand piano.

Ludwig sat down and played a few runs and chords. "What a beautiful instrument! Even practicing here will be wonderful."

The Lichnowskys took their seats on a small couch. Elise and Ludwig sat down together and played the sonata for four hands. Their listeners watched and listened intently. What they witnessed was a flawless presentation by two musicians who worked together with immaculate precision. There was nothing mechanical about their play. It was two minds working together, entirely focused on the music they were bringing to life together.

The countess looked at her husband. She held a fan in front of her face and whispered, "I cannot believe that she has been taught by him only for a short time! They are playing like they have been doing it for years."

Quietly he replied, "It is something truly extraordinary. Perfect unity! It will be a great concert and a surprise to everybody who will be there. He will go far in the world, but she will also make herself a name as a musician!"

Ludwig's face looked pleased when they were finished. He pointed out a few passages that they repeated. Ludwig played an amusing piece that he had prepared, the Rondo a Capriccio, which had been dubbed the *Rage over the Lost Penny*. It was a piece that Elise had suggested. She had laughed when she'd explained why he should present it. "This one really sticks out. You wrote it after getting so terribly upset over this coin that you lost in the house quite a while back. Remember how you cursed and swore? I just think that it really paints a picture of you. It is almost like making fun of yourself: hello, this is Ludwig van Beethoven when he flies into a rage. Watch out, everybody!"

They both found it amusing. "And why not?" He had grinned. "I think that's exactly how I will announce this piece! You always have these amazing ideas, Elise!"

The Lichnowskys applauded enthusiastically after he finished playing the piece. "What a lot of humor! This will be a fun piece for everybody," commented the prince. He looked at his pocket watch. "It's time for me to retire for the night. I also don't want to spoil the surprise for tomorrow. I expect that you'll still have pieces to discuss and practice. Feel free to do so, and good night!" The Lichnowskys left the concert room.

Elise and Ludwig stayed behind. "Let's take another look at the sonata that you thought was wonderful to play on a moonlit evening," suggested Ludwig. Elise agreed. For her, it was the highlight of her presentation. The piece attracted her as much as ever, and she put everything she had into it. There was the dreamy, quiet movement, which conveyed gentleness and longing; the carefree, dance-like middle movement; and the final movement, which was dynamic, unrestrained, and passionate.

Ludwig waited till she had finished playing the entire piece. She looked up, wondering whether she had played this masterpiece the way he had envisaged it. He did not say a word. Instead of answering her unspoken question, he enfolded her in his embrace and cradled her against his chest. She heard his heartbeat, felt the warmth of his body, and let herself sink into the depth of his gaze. The candles were burning lower and cast their flickering light into the silent room.

"Elise..." He buried his face in her hair and covered her face with his kisses. "You have played this piece the way I feel it. I also felt all the love you put into it." His mouth was on hers, gentle and tender at first, then hot and demanding. She felt herself surrender to his passion as it matched her own, and she kissed him back. Out of breath, they got up. He carried the candlestick with the last burning candle in one hand and put his other arm around her as they tiptoed along the hallway to their rooms.

"We have to get some sleep," he murmured. "But I don't know how I can fall asleep, Elise." He held her tight, and she could not let go of him either. In the last flickering light, she leaned into him, and he looked at her lips, which were waiting for his.

"I can't sleep either, Ludwig," she whispered. She saw the ardent, unrestrained passion in his eyes and felt his kisses fueling her own burning desire for him even more. Their souls, their minds felt like one, and they both felt the urgency and need for physical closeness. Silently, she opened the door to her room, and he swept her into his arms.

Elise woke up at dawn. Beside her, she heard the deep and regular breathing of Ludwig. She curled up beside him. He stirred and put his arms around her. "Too early to get up," he mumbled sleepily. But then his eyes opened cautiously. "Maybe I should pretend to be an example of high morals and go to my room. After all, this is my friends' place, and the countess's sister is a mother superior." His face had a naughty smile, and he hugged Elise.

She giggled and gave him a quick kiss. "I don't know what they would think of us if they knew about last night...yes, it's probably better, or we'll both lose our last shred of good reputation."

Quietly he left, and Elise fell asleep again. The morning noises of the household woke her up. Servants were walking along the hallways, and there was a clatter of dishes from the kitchen. She did not know what time it was, but she jumped out of bed. Quickly she washed herself and got dressed. She looked into the gilded wall mirror and saw a face that looked glowingly happy. Quickly she brushed her hair and turned it into a fashionable, upswept style.

She went to the drawing room. Ludwig's friends eyed her with approval. "It looks like you had a good rest," Lady Lichnowsky remarked. "Being in Vienna becomes you! And this dress looks absolutely charming on you." She stepped aside and handed Elise the other dresses that the seamstress had adjusted for her.

The prince looked at his watch. "Ludwig seems to be the sleepyhead this morning. I think I'll go and whisper the word 'coffee' into his ear. Knowing him that should wake him up really fast." He went down the hallway, and within a short time Ludwig appeared. Elise knew that he could emerge from his room in record time in the mornings, decently dressed, with his unruly hair in remarkable order.

He entered and offered an apologetic smile. "I hope that I am not holding everybody up with breakfast?"

They laughed. "There is no rush, dear friend. We know that you are not up with the birds, but you stay up with the owls."

The group had a cheerful, relaxed mood. The morning was cooler, and a fire burned in the tiled stove and cast comfortable warmth into the room. Conversation flowed easily, and it was obvious that Ludwig's friends enjoyed their visitors. Elise's concern that she would feel out of place or confused in the Vienna of 1802 disappeared like the fall fog had disappeared in the morning sun.

They went for a pleasant stroll in a nearby park later. The day seemed to fly by. After supper everybody got ready for the concert. Elise quickly went to her room to change into the dress Lady Lichnowsky had suggested. As she stepped into the hallway, she almost collided with Ludwig, who quickly caught her by her arm. "Don't run so fast," he teased. "I need at least one kiss before the concert!"

Exuberantly, she threw her arms around his neck. "Yes, but not only one. For good luck at the concert, Ludwig."

He held her. "Look at you! You look absolutely stunning!"

She smiled at him. "And you are so dressed up that nobody in Heiligenstadt would even recognize you! Just one thing…you forgot to comb your hair!" He made a funny face at her as he corrected this problem. Together, they entered the concert hall.

Elise looked with surprise at the crowd of people that had gathered. It was clearly not only a concert for the Lichnowskys but also for their large circle of friends. When they entered, the steady hum of the conversation subsided, and people turned to look at them.

The prince rose to address the audience. "Friends, I feel very honored by every one of you who came to our evening concert, thank you! I also feel very privileged to have Mr. Ludwig van Beethoven here today. He is my valued friend and, as you are very likely aware of, one of the great musicians here in Vienna. We feel very fortunate that he moved to our city just over ten years ago. One of his very promising, talented students, Elise Helfing, is going to present some of his works as well. We are starting with a piano sonata for four hands. Give your appreciation to the artists who are about to entertain you!"

Applause sounded through the hall as Ludwig and Elise went to the instrument and stood to bow slightly before the audience. They took their seats and started to play. Their personal style of playing blended into a flawless performance. Elise forgot that there was a big audience. She felt no fear that critical tongues would discuss the music and their play. It was like an invisible shelter surrounded her and Ludwig. Together they were infusing life into one of his works, and nothing else seemed to matter.

The hall became so silent that one could have heard the rustle of a dress. The audience followed with breathless attention. As they finished, there was a wave of applause and shouts of "Bravo!"

Ludwig prepared to present his Rondo a Capriccio. With a short wave of his hand, he silenced the applause that greeted him. "This piece has another name. It is called *Rage over the Lost Penny*. A very dear friend has characterized it as a musical sketch that depicts me." He laughed. "I may not be a good observer of myself; that's why we need dear friends who are watching us. So, here comes Ludwig van Beethoven—watch out! The man could have one of his infamous tempers. But not today, of course…I promise that I'll be on my best behavior."

There was laughter from the listeners. They had not expected that. He played the piece to the captivated audience, and roaring applause sounded through the room at the end. Other pieces followed, and the prince announced the last presentation. "My friends, the artist left the best for the last point of the evening. You are about to witness the first ever performance of a new piano sonata. It is written like a fantasy."

There was a murmuring in the audience when Elise went to the piano. Ludwig stood up. "You may be surprised that it is not me, the composer, who is performing this work today, but after hearing Elise play this piece, I made the choice that she should present it. She has an outstanding ability to feel the expression of this piece, and I would not do it any different." The murmuring stopped, and there was applause. Elise played the sonata, painting the mood of every movement. All eyes were on her, and surprised glances were exchanged.

The Lichnowskys were fascinated by the performance. The countess's glance also went over to Ludwig. She noted that his eyes were riveted on Elise. Elise was entirely focused on every section of the piece, but between the movements she paused, and her glance seemed to lock with Ludwig's intent gaze. The connection was almost tangible. Lady Lichnowsky quietly touched the hand of her husband. "Look at them—it is like two souls that are one."

Thoughtfully, he looked, smiled at his wife, and, with silent understanding, held her hand.

Thundering applause started when the last note was finished. There were shouts of "Bravo" and the stomping of feet. Ludwig went to the piano and joined Elise. "We are going to play another sonata for four hands to conclude the evening."

They sat down, and the audience turned quiet. There was more applause after they had finished the upbeat last movement, which was like a happy and exuberant game of catch that the bass and the soprano played together. After that the concert guests still lingered. They spoke to Ludwig. He seemed to know some of them. Several guests commissioned music pieces, and Ludwig made a quick note of their names and requests.

Numerous concertgoers surrounded Elise. They wanted to know how long she had received music instruction, and there were gasps of surprise when they heard that she had been working under Ludwig's guidance only for a few months. Others wanted to know when there would be another concert.

Finally, the last guests left. Servants appeared and put the chairs away, and Ludwig, Elise, and the Lichnowskys sat together in the drawing room. Prince Lichnowsky was the first one to speak. "What a wonderful evening! This will be remembered by us and by all our friends for a long time! I love music, but the way you, Ludwig, are creating these pieces is nothing short of a miracle to me. And the way you are working together is like magic. What is even more incredible is the fact that Elise has been your student only for a relatively short time."

The countess added, "I believe that I have never seen such a connection between two musicians before—tell me if I am wrong!"

Ludwig and Elise exchanged glances before Ludwig replied. "Your observation is true, Countess. Elise is a very insightful and perceptive lady. She loves music, and as you work together, you can find that a piece of music truly unites the artists. As a result, working together can be not only a source of satisfaction but also a source of great joy."

There was silence. Elise felt that there were many more questions that the Lichnowskys wanted to ask, but Ludwig had been very diplomatic in his answer. This was all he wanted to reveal, and it was obvious that they did not want to intrude or pry. The countess rose. "The music of this evening will follow me into my dreams—wonderful pieces! It has been a lot of work for you. You must be tired."

Ludwig responded, "Well, concerts are stimulating! As a result, after a concert I'm usually fired up. Didn't you call me a night owl this morning? Will it disturb you if I'm still playing some music?"

The prince raised his hands. "Goodness, no! You were still practicing yesterday, and it was a most pleasant way for me to listen to music and fall asleep to it. Just don't thunder away with some wild tunes! We all know that Ludwig can have a wild temper in his music."

Ludwig put his hands on his heart. "I promise that it will be something calm, reflective, and suitable for this hour of the evening—thank you! And I don't think that I'll carry on for hours. That would be abusing your generous hospitality!" The Lichnowskys said good night and left.

Ludwig stretched on his seat. "Elise, it has been a long day. Are you too tired to listen to more music?"

"I'm never too tired to listen to music, especially your music." She looked at him with those clear, bright eyes that had become so dear to him. It was a look of love that shook him to the core. "You seem to be looking into my soul again, my love. I'll play one piece for you. It's not on paper yet, but it is in my mind."

He started to weave a soft melody. It sounded like a nocturne. Elise's eyes opened wide. She knew the piece, as Mark had played it a while back. It was the "Andante Favori" in F major. She listened to the melody, which was soothing and calming; it went on a playful excursion but reflected the mood of an evening and the night. She was not entirely familiar with the piece but knew enough to analyze its course and feel when it was close to the finish. Silently she moved to the piano and stood beside Ludwig.

As he finished playing the piece, he looked away from the keys of the instrument into her face, his eyes embracing her, yearning for her. Elise leaned her head against his shoulder and said, "I think I understand what you want to tell me with your music, and I see the question in your eyes. Yes, Ludwig, I love you too."

His voice was raw with emotion and desire for her. "Oh, my love! I have been waiting for this moment all evening." He pulled her into his arms, and she felt herself melt into his embrace. Did she walk, or did he carry her through the quiet hallway to her room? She did not know; she just felt herself sinking, held by his arms, feeling his mouth and savoring his tenderness and the fulfillment of their togetherness. Faint daylight was dawning when they finally fell asleep in each other's arms.

A little while later, Ludwig sat up. He stroked her cheek. "Just for the sake of the house rules, I'll go and pretend that I have slept in my bed," he whispered.

"I know," she murmured sleepily, "better not spoil things with your friends. Will you wake me up if I sleep in?"

"Of course, just go back to sleep!" The door closed soundlessly.

Elise woke up to soft knocking on her door. She shot out of bed and hurried to get dressed. Her sleeping in...that was kind of embarrassing! Would they suspect anything? A look in the mirror calmed her concerns. She did not look like a person that had celebrated all night long and almost forgotten to sleep!

There was a trace of embarrassment in her face as she entered the dining room, but the Lichnowskys wished her a cordial good morning. Everybody was in a relaxed and happy mood. Ludwig smiled. "Elise feels guilty for sleeping in, because it is she who is always up early in Heiligenstadt."

Elise's embarrassment subsided. "You guessed right. I feel very spoiled here—like a princess. This is straight out of a fairy tale."

The group laughed. Lady Lichnowsky gave her a cordial smile. "And you deserve it. Why don't you just enjoy?"

Elise and Ludwig decided to travel back to Heiligenstadt in the early afternoon hours. The Lichnowskys insisted that their driver would bring them back to the village. The Lichnowskys also pointed out that it would be so much more convenient for them to travel in the chaise than in the cramped coach. Before they left, the prince handed a small bag with coins to Ludwig. "You have given us a most memorable evening. Take this as our token of thanks!" He turned to Elise and handed her a gold coin, a ducat.

"You are way too generous!" Elise was slightly overwhelmed.

The prince laughed. "No, not at all! The pleasure has been all ours."

As they sat in the chaise, they felt they could stay in a world of their own. Ludwig held Elise in his arm. "I am the happiest person, but there is sadness too."

Elise looked at him questioningly. "Where does the sadness come from?"

"I would love to marry you, Elise, but I'm just a musician who is starting to get a name. I cannot even give you all the things a wife would expect: a house, servants, a comfortable life, jewels, clothes…"

Elise shook her head. "Ludwig, you have been giving me more than I have ever dreamed of. Not every woman has a partner who is loving and devoted." She seemed to be looking back, far back, in her memories. "Take my father: he gave my mother a huge diamond ring and insisted that he wanted to marry her. He wanted her like somebody wants to have something to brag about. My mother was fit for this: she was good-looking, smart, and had a lot of friends. He was charming and good-looking, I was told, but otherwise he seemed to be selfish and not a caring person at all.

"My mother got pregnant, and there was a baby—that was me. He was not thrilled at the prospect of fatherhood, as a child did not fit into his plans. He lived his life and was never home. She did not know where he was, but friends of hers saw him with other women. And one day he packed his clothes and left her a note. That was all. He said that he was done. He never wanted children, and he wanted his freedom. So it was my mother who raised me. She loved me very much."

Ludwig seemed to be thinking of a faraway time as well. He started, "I had a loving mother too. She passed away when I was seventeen years old, and that was much too early. My younger brother was only thirteen at that time. My father sought solace in drinking after her death, which, of course, only made matters worse. He had never been an easy person to get along with in the first place. Also he had been fond of drinking and celebrating before, and my mother had been holding the family together. He lost his work. When she passed away, everything just started to fall apart, his life and the life of the family. I went back to look after the family's needs for a while, but then I came back to Vienna for good, and my brother settled in Vienna too. It is over. I remember it as a difficult time."

Ludwig gave her a comforting embrace. "That's just a glimpse of my life some years back. It is getting better. I'm getting more commissioned work, performing more concerts. I love you, but I am not much of a provider at this point."

Elise looked at him and shrugged her shoulders. "This should not bother you at all. For starters, stop paying me as your housekeeper. Save your money.

You are teaching me, and with more knowledge I can be a music teacher and earn money too."

He looked at her with astonishment. "You have incredibly unconventional ideas. Women are usually considered weak and in need of protection."

Elise laughed. "Look who is calling somebody unconventional! Didn't you tell me that you think that people should be equal? Doesn't this apply to women too? I heard that there are women poets and women musicians. So I can be one too! And being against rules and convention, you told me that you had some conservative characters getting upset with you because you didn't make a deep bow before nobility."

He gave her an affectionate squeeze. "Aha! You caught me again! Yes, I admit it: convention is bothersome to me. But there are responsibilities. I could never live with myself abandoning the woman I loved if she were to become pregnant with my child."

Elise nodded. "Yes, Ludwig, I know how you feel, and I love you and trust you."

He thought for a moment before saying, "This village, Heiligenstadt, is very small. Everybody seems to talk about everybody. I don't want you to get into the meanspirited gossip of the people. It is almost time that I go back to Vienna, and people in the big city are a lot more tolerant of a young lady living at the same place with a man, even if they are not married yet."

Elise smiled. "I am not worried, Ludwig. Let them talk, if they really have nothing better to do with their lives. Look at this example: my mother is divorced from my father. You know that he abandoned her. She has a very nice gentleman friend, and he lives with her at our place. At one point they want to get married, but nobody calls my mom a whore because of her current living arrangement. Times are changing."

Ludwig looked at her with astonishment. "You have thoughts that are beyond our time. I guess we are similar; I collide with the conservative forces in music. You are challenging the ideas of convention, and you have been called a revolutionary. Different ideas give us freedom, and yet struggling for freedom can be difficult..."

"But it is worth it," added Elise, and they moved closer together on their seat as they drove through the countryside.

Ten

Fall and a Rainy Night

The chaise rolled along the village street of Heiligenstadt and stopped in front of the old farmhouse. The driver helped to carry the travel bags to the door, and Ludwig thanked him and gave him a tip. The vehicle rumbled off, and as they stood in front of the door, he smiled at her. "I feel like I want to carry you across the threshold."

Elise did not protest. She clasped her hands behind his neck, and he carried her into the living area and shoved the bedroom door open with his boot. Together they fell onto the bed. He kissed her with his eyes. "Dearest Elise, this is not Vienna! How I wish I could offer you all the luxury that surrounded us there for the last few days."

Elise shook her head. "No, Ludwig, don't think like that. Happiness can live in small and simple places. Luxury is no guarantee for happiness."

They forgot the world around them. The sun had set, and a blue, gentle evening light filtered into the room. He got up, lit a few candles, and put them into the candle holders on the dresser. They lay close together, and he caressed her face and her body. "I could stay like that forever," he sighed, and she gently drew the line of his face, his chin, and his lips like she wanted to embed his features forever in her memory.

There was a knock at the door and a shout. "Mr. Ludwig! Oh, Mr. Ludwig!"

He cursed and quickly got out of bed, searching for his clothes. "Better stay," he whispered to her. "I'll go and see what is happening." He replied loudly, "Yes! I'm home. Who is there?"

They heard the neighbor's voice. Moser-Marie was at the door. "You forgot your travel bags! They are still standing at the door."

"Oh, I forgot about those! Thank you. I'll be right there." He hurried to give his clothes a semblance of order, brushed back his tousled hair, and went to the door.

Moser-Marie handed him the bags. "Better take them in. It could rain in the night."

"Oh, yes, of course. I just totally forgot. Thank you for...uh...reminding me!" He seemed to be at a loss for words as he absent-mindedly grabbed the luggage.

Moser-Marie was shaking her head as she left. What had happened to this man? Usually he was so particular about his belongings. He did not seem to be drunk, but he acted like she had woken him up in the middle of the night—so totally oblivious! Also, why had his housekeeper not brought the bags inside? Where was Elise? She had not seen the girl for a few days. Had she taken off, like the previous helper? But this did not make sense either, as things had been going well for her! Moser-Marie went back to the other side of the house, thoroughly puzzled.

Elise sat up as Ludwig returned, and he sat down beside her. "Too bad that this interrupted our quiet evening for a bit."

Elise laughed. "Thanks for checking the door! I couldn't have done that in my state of total undress. That would have been something to get the rumor-mill running." As she looked out into the waning daylight, she remarked, "It is getting dark and cold. I should go and get some water and start a fire."

"Just get a bit of water. We don't need much. I'll start the fire. Is there anything in the house to eat?"

Elise made a face. "Your housekeeper was on a vacation in Vienna...I'm just making a joke, of course! There is not much food in the house, but there is enough to make a soup." Quickly she put on her plain, country-style dress and went to the fountain across from the house. Nobody was there to ask any questions, for which she was glad. It would be something she might have to deal with on another occasion.

When she returned, they sat together at the table. The warming fire cast a cozy glow. Elise had done some cleaning up, and Ludwig looked at her cautiously. "I hope you are not saying good night and climbing up those stairs to the room upstairs?"

Elise moved closer to him. "It depends on what you want. If you want your space, I'll go upstairs."

He held on to her hand. "No, don't go," he replied quickly. "Besides, it will be cold up there, and this bed here is probably a bit more comfortable."

"What if I am up early tomorrow?"

He smiled. "Don't worry; I sleep deeply. And you don't have to be up so early every day. I don't even know how you do that!" Ludwig yawned and stretched. "I think I'll call it a day." He stripped off his day clothes, and they curled up under the covers close together.

⌒

*D*aylight was shining into the window when Elise woke up. It felt like she had slept in. With a start she realized that the sun shone so brightly into the bedroom window that it must be late. The church clock in the distance chimed nine times. Ludwig was still asleep, and she cautiously got out of bed and tiptoed around to get her clothes. She had to get the day started, as there was a lot to do after the days in Vienna. In the kitchen she began to make the morning coffee. The water in the buckets was precariously low, and she flew out of the door to replenish the supply.

Moser-Marie stood under her door at the other side of the house as Elise darted by. "Good morning, Elise! Oh, you are back—I haven't seen you in a few days."

Elise stopped in her tracks. This was the last thing she needed! She was late with everything this morning, and here was the neighbor, who was in the mood for a chat. But she realized that nothing would be gained by hurrying. "Yes, Moser-Marie. We came back from Vienna yesterday!"

The neighbor gave her a questioning glance. "Vienna? That's quite a distance to travel. What did you do?"

"Mr. Ludwig had been invited to give a concert, and his friends—you know the lady who brought me here and her husband—they invited me too."

Moser-Marie put her hands on her hips. "Well, that's a step up from our little village. Good for you that you went along too! Did you enjoy yourself?"

It was a simple enough question, but it made Elise search for words. How could she describe those days? It had been a time beyond her dreams, and the memories were giving her wings. She took a deep breath. "Oh, it was—not because this was the big city—it was just…well, even saying wonderful is not enough."

The older woman looked into Elise's face. The girl seemed to be in another world. She saw a glow of happiness in Elise's face, and she knew. She had seen it in her daughters' faces when they had fallen in love. It had been as plainly written on their faces as it was now on the face of this girl. Also, like pieces of a puzzle, everything that she had found bewildering last evening fell into place: Mr. Ludwig's absent-minded behavior, leaving the luggage behind outside, and Elise being up and about late today. "Oh, Elise, no need to say more. I understand." Her eyes were full of knowledge and wisdom. "I wish you all the happiness, and I wish the same to Mr. Ludwig. Also I want you to know that nobody in the neighborhood will hear of our conversation." There was the smallest note of sadness in her voice. "I feel that you will not stay here much longer. You and Mr. Ludwig will move to Vienna, of course. I will miss you."

"Yes, and thank you, Moser-Marie. He has talked about moving to Vienna, but we don't know when."

Elise went back to the house. Ludwig was in the living area. "I hope the neighbor did not put you through something like the Spanish Inquisition," he commented.

"No, she is not one of those individuals. But I told her that we had a concert in Vienna. And she figured that you would not be staying here much longer."

"Ah, the sixth sense of women!" Ludwig nodded.

Elise calmed his concerns. "She promised that this piece of news would not make its rounds in the village." They sat down for a quick breakfast, after which Ludwig worked on a composition. Elise hurried to the market to purchase some basic supplies. Some neighbor women accosted her about her absence, but all they could get out of her was a quick statement that she had been invited to a concert in Vienna and it had been a beautiful event. This seemed to be enough for them, and there were no further questions.

When Elise returned, she found Ludwig sitting at the piano. "This is something that I started writing a long time ago. It's a song, and somehow I put it away. It did not seem to be meaningful enough to me at that point to get it to a publisher." He intoned a few bars of the beginning. "The words are not my lyrics. A man, Karl Friedrich Wilhelm Herrosee wrote the words sometime back, but I wrote a melody for them."

He looked at her as his thoughts went back. "When I set the words to music, I was not in love. I was intrigued by the text, as it conveyed the message of how love can be a source of comfort and how people who are truly in love can share joys and sorrows. I was about twenty when I wrote it, hoping that one day I would find a woman with whom I would share my joys and sorrows. Those were the dreams of a very young man. And as it was so far away from reality, I put this piece away, almost forgot about it. But now this song has meaning for me, because of you, my dear! We both have joy—great joy, but we also have our burdens and sorrows."

Elise sat down expectantly. He started to play and sang the song for her:
I love you as you love me,
in the evening and the morning,
nor was there a day when you and I
did not share our troubles.

And when we shared them
they became easier to bear;
you comforted me in my distress,
and I wept in your laments.

Therefore, may God's blessing be upon you,
You, my life's joy.
God protect you, keep you for me,
and protect and keep us both.

She came to the piano and put her arms around him. "You have given me the most precious gift I have ever received—oh, Ludwig!" He held her in his arms. Then she looked at him intently. "Ludwig, I love you, and this song is one of the most beautiful love songs that exists. Even though you said that I have given the song meaning for you, I think it is time that you take it to a publisher.

Everybody will love this piece! It has to be shared. You can't let it sit around in a drawer between your clothes and stockings. This has to come out and make its way into the world!"

Ludwig agreed. "You are seeing the practical side of things, which is often overlooked by the artist. And—God knows—I'm not the most organized individual anyways! So I write pieces and put them away…but, yes, it has to go to a publisher now! I'll call it "Tender Love.""

Ludwig looked out the window. "It looks like a beautiful afternoon for a walk through the fields. You know my routine of strolling through the area, and then I come back with muddy boots. There was no rain, so the path will be better. It would even be suitable for less than sturdy boots. Would you want to come along?"

Elise was happy to join him. He mused, "There is just one small problem. People usually start talking if a man and a woman go for a walk together. Aren't you concerned about that?"

Elise shook her head. "I mentioned it to you before: let them talk if they have nothing better to do. It is no crime to go for a walk together. And if they want to gossip, they'll find something even if we are not walking together. They'll speculate about what's going on inside the house!"

Resolutely she put on her shoes, and they went along the road to the fields. A few curious glances followed them from behind curtained windows. As they walked, they breathed in the clear air. He had to think about the difference between this country setting and Vienna. "It has been beautiful here. Clear air, clear skies…It is quieter than Vienna, less driven, less hectic. But somehow there is a time for everything. It's time to think about going back to Vienna." He looked expectantly at Elise. "Are you looking forward to leaving, or will you miss the village?"

Elise stopped walking. "Ludwig, I look forward to the next part of the journey. No, I won't miss the village. I'll go wherever you want to go." She paused. "As long as you want me to be there." They stood in the field under the clear fall sky and embraced.

In the distance a shepherd was tending a flock of sheep. He carried a wooden flute with him, and Elise noticed that he started to play his instrument to entertain himself. She tried to catch the tune he was playing.

"What are you listening to, Elise?" Ludwig did not seem to hear the sound of the flute.

It hit Elise like a lightning bolt that she was witnessing how his hearing was deteriorating. Of course, she had read about this, but now she was living in the painful reality. Ludwig's hearing loss was present. It affected him. Living through it was different than just reading about the bare facts in a historical book. She tried to sound unconcerned. "I'm just watching the shepherd over there." She pointed to the figure in the distance. "He is playing his flute." She heard the simple folk tune loud and clear.

Ludwig shook his head. "I'm afraid I don't hear him. Yes, I see though that he is playing."

Elise resorted to a white lie. She did not like to do it, but she also did not want to see Ludwig more distressed than he already was. "It's not very clear, as he is far away," she added.

Ludwig was silent but was obviously preoccupied. After a while he spoke up, "It's my hearing problem. It's the buzzing sound in my ears, and also I find it difficult to hear things as clearly as I would like to. My doctor wanted to see me again. I think I'll see him soon. He wanted me to take the waters till fall, and so I'd better do that."

Elise encouraged him. "I believe that you are feeling better than in the beginning of summer. You seem to be more rested—at least that's what I seem to observe."

"Yes," he agreed. "I feel better. I'm ready to work again in Vienna. There is work waiting for me. I can go back to it now. It is time. Somehow I'm worried that the feeling of being well is not going to last, and the curative waters have not helped with my hearing problem. All of this is a source of concern to me."

They found a wild apple tree and picked some of the fruit. "It's fall, and there are no flowers to bring home." He sounded disappointed, but Elise pointed to the colorful foliage of a maple tree and the vibrant berries on a mountain ash tree.

"There is beauty in everything, Ludwig; it does not matter which season. Let's take some branches to the house."

He agreed. "Thank you for reminding me. I may not be able to hear as well as I'd like to, but I should be grateful for the gift of sight and all the other gifts of living." Hand in hand, they walked back to the farmhouse.

L udwig had left in the morning to go to the bathhouse. He had continued taking the waters for a few weeks, and he also wanted to have
another consultation with the physician. Elise was busy with the work that
had to be done every day. The days had turned cooler, and a brisk wind was
blowing. It was definitely not the time to be outdoors all day. She opened the
kitchen windows to air out the woodsmoke from the stove but was grateful
when she could close them again. There had been a rain shower the night
before, and it was cool and damp outside, so the heat of the stove was needed
to keep the house comfortable.

Ludwig opened the door and entered the house. His face brightened
when he looked at her, but he sat down heavily on a chair and was quiet and
preoccupied.

"Ludwig?" she asked.

"Yes, my love, I'm back." He sighed. "I should not have gone and seen
the doctor. He really had no advice for me—just told me that the hearing
problem is something I will have to live with. And, of course, he does not
guarantee that taking curative waters will put a stop to feeling unwell." He
looked depressed, defeated.

Elise sat down next to him and held his hands, which were nervously
moving about. "Ludwig, as you said before, doctors are not all knowing.
So what he has been telling you is just like a picture in time. We simply
cannot know what the future will hold. But life is now. You cannot allow
yourself to live in fear of what will be. We all have to live now, one day at
a time."

He looked at her. There was intense pain in his eyes, but underneath was
a faint glimmer of hope and a will to fight. "Life has to go on."

Several days later, they had been playing some music together and enjoying it. It was late in the afternoon. The windy fall day had turned drizzly,
and dark clouds were billowing in the windswept sky. Ludwig went to his
writing desk. A few blank sheets of paper were lying around. Elise quickly
glanced over to him. He was not writing music today. It looked like he was
working on a letter. It was not often that he was busy with correspondence,
but he had relatives and friends in Vienna. From what she observed, writing
letters—at least composing this letter—did not seem to come easy to him.

He interrupted his writing frequently to think. At one point he took a page and ripped it into pieces.

Elise went outside into the backyard to collect some kitchen herbs. Later she ventured to the fountain. A few women were gathered and talking together. She offered them a friendly greeting, and in return, there were a few inquisitive glances. One woman frankly stared at her. "Not a nice day to walk in the fields, girl? Of course, it's cozier inside the house with a man in bed?"

Elise gave her an even look. She tossed back her head. "No, today is not a good day to enjoy a walk and some fresh air, whether it's alone or in company. But bad weather does not seem to be a hindrance to you spreading rumors and gossip at the fountain?"

The woman looked indignantly at Elise. "Oh, just stop playing the innocent! I saw you walking with that musician a few days ago. Walking way out in the fields too and coming home when it was almost nightfall! Ha! Some housekeeper, I must say! What other services are you offering?" Viciously she spat out the words.

Contemptuously, Elise looked at her. "Your imagination is running wild. Maybe everybody here should start asking you a few questions about what you were doing when you were younger."

The woman laughed loudly. "Well, I certainly never was a whore to some musician—"

A voice cut her short. "Save your poison, Rosa! This is enough! How dare you insult this girl with your vulgar remarks! Shame on you!" Moser-Marie had joined the group and witnessed the vicious words of the woman.

Rosa was not ready to stop. "We don't need people like that in this village. And you, Moser-Marie, you are just turning a blind eye because you are harboring this scum in your house, and, of course, this—"

Without a word, Moser-Marie dipped her bucket into the fountain, but instead of carrying it home, she poured it over the head of the woman. Rosa was soaking wet, and her last few words were just a blubber through the cascade of water that had been poured over her.

The others did not offer her much sympathy. They actually laughed! She seemed to be known for her viciousness. "Go home, Rosa! Maybe the clean water will wash some of the filth out of your language! Go home, sit at the stove, and dry off."

Elise went back to the house. She knew that Moser-Marie was a person who would not make her or Ludwig's life miserable with vicious remarks. But she knew that there were mean spirited individuals, and the village was small.

"You took a while getting water. I started to worry about you." His glance searched her face. "What happened?"

Elise told him about the encounter with the gossipy woman. "They are just small-minded people," he said evenly, "but I feel bad that this happened to you." His face showed anger. "Maybe I should give this primitive shred of humanity a piece of my mind!" Furiously he jumped up from his chair, ready to dash out of the house.

Elise held him back. "No, Ludwig, don't! Stay here!"

He was angry. "She implied that you are a whore and that we are scum! Do you think I'll let this insult sit? I have my pride!"

"It's all taken care of. Our neighbor Moser-Marie came to the fountain when she was in the middle of her tirade. And when she did not stop, Moser-Marie poured a bucket of water over her head. That did it. What a way to cool her down! The others know her already as a meanspirited woman, and they laughed at her and said that they hoped that the clean water would wash the filth out of her language."

Ludwig relented. "I will leave it. But all the same, I think our time here in this village is just about up. And when we are in Vienna, it will be time that we get married!"

He was still busy writing during the evening. Elise did not ask any questions. It had to be something of importance to him, and he probably would feel relieved when he was finished writing the letter.

The next day brought more rain. "I think I'll order a coach for us for to-morrow," Ludwig said. "It will give me time to get everything ready for the move back to Vienna."

Elise was not surprised. The idea of going to Vienna was rather a relief. She was prepared to go with him. For her, there was not much to pack up. She went through Ludwig's belongings together with him. Music sheets were packed into a box. A wooden chest held his clothing and personal belongings. The housekeeping items stayed at the house.

*L*udwig went out to order a coach. Elise stayed behind. On his desk was a lengthy document; it was the letter he had been writing. Elise went over to the desk. There was an undercurrent of fear in her. He had been in such a dark mood. This was not a letter that had come easy. The way he had paused to think, the way his facial expression had been, it must have been difficult for him to pen it down. She started to read. It was not easy for her, as it was written in the old-fashioned handwriting of 1802, but she persisted. It got easier for her as she gradually got used to deciphering the script.

She held her breath as she read the lines. It was like a cry of despair. She knew that he would turn deaf, but this document was so tangible that it drove her to tears. Feverishly, she read on:

FOR MY BROTHERS CARL AND JOHANN BEETHOVEN

OH! Ye who think or declare me to be hostile, morose, and misanthropic, how unjust you are, and how little you know the secret cause of what appears thus to you! My heart and mind were ever from childhood prone to feelings of affection, and I was always disposed to accomplish something great. But you must remember that six years ago I was attacked by an incurable malady, aggravated by unskillful physicians, deluded from year to year, too, by the hope of relief, and at length forced to the conviction of a lasting affliction (the cure of which may go on for years, and perhaps after all prove impracticable).

Born with a passionate and excitable temperament, keenly susceptible to the pleasures of society, I was yet obliged early in life to isolate myself, and to pass my existence in solitude. If I at any time resolved to surmount all this, oh! How cruelly was I again repelled by the experience, sadder than ever, of my defective hearing! And yet I found it impossible to say to others:

"Speak louder; shout! For I am deaf!" Alas…

Elise's hands trembled as she tried to read on; the writing blurred in front of her eyes as tears streamed down her face. Here was a written document that dealt with his despair and resignation. It was an effort for her to continue, and yet she could not stop reading. She had to know the full truth. The tone of this letter became more and more desperate. It sounded like he considered putting an end to his life. He knew that he had an incurable condition and the final stage would be deafness. Of course, he had voiced his fears to her earlier. She remembered that evening when he had sat in front of her like a condemned man and she had tried to make him see beyond the difficulties he had described. And now he had put his despair on paper, despair so profound that it was driving him to the brink of harming himself.

With a flash of clarity, she realized that she was reading Ludwig's Heiligenstadt Testament. It had been a subject of history. She had read the letter in a book about musical history. But here was the original version, so direct and tangible that it shook her up beyond control. Quickly she walked away from the desk and washed her face. She could not let him see the tears she had cried. He was preoccupied with suicide, with ending it all. He simply could not do that!

All of a sudden she realized why she was here in Heiligenstadt, first in a convent and now with Ludwig. She had told Sister Martha that her life was changing and challenged Sister Martha to embrace the change, to follow her heart and live her life to its fullest. She had encouraged Josepha to be in charge of her life and refuse to say yes to a fate that had been decided for her by her parents. She had told Josepha that she owed it to herself to make her own choices. Next she had been thrown into the role of a housekeeper for Ludwig van Beethoven and had become much more, a student and a lover. It was up to her to tell him that this letter should never be sent to his family members. It would cause them immense grief. His suicide would be devastating!

She had to get him to think, to accept, and to choose. Yes, it was all about making choices again, choices that would steer the direction of a life. He had to accept that his work was not finished. His life was a gift to him. His gift of music was a gift to the world that would endure for centuries to come. He owed it to himself and to the world to live his life and fight the obstacles, even if at times they seemed insurmountable. She would stay with him till her mission was fulfilled. Was this the future? Was this the purpose of her existence now? Never mind the future…She closed her eyes and took a deep breath as she accepted this task and the responsibilities that were ahead of her.

Ludwig came back after one hour. Elise busied herself with some more work at the house. He seemed less preoccupied, as everything had been arranged for the trip back to Vienna. "We need music in our lives," he remarked. "Tomorrow the driver will pick up the piano and transport it back to Vienna." "What are you wanting to play?" Elise wondered. His smile embraced her lovingly. "Can't you guess? We created a piece together, *Für Elise*. He started to play, and when he was finished, he handed her the finished music score, which was now tidily written out and bore a dedication to her.

"You have a way of overwhelming me, Ludwig." Thankfully she kissed him.

"And, of course, there is the other piece, which you described as something that depicts a moonlit evening—your personal favorite." He moved over. "Here, you play it! You do it exactly the way I had imagined it."

Elise started playing. There was a knock at the door. Moser-Marie stood at the entrance. Perplexed, she looked at Elise. "I always thought you were simply a housekeeper. You are a wonderful musician. I can't believe it!"

Ludwig smiled at her. "Yes, Elise is a wonderful person!"

Moser-Marie continued. "I just wanted to wish you all the best, as you will be moving away. Come and call on us if you are back in Heiligenstadt. We will be out tomorrow all day, getting the beehives ready for winter, and so I came by this evening! Here are some candles for your place in Vienna. It is something to remember us by when you light them in Vienna, and we wish you happiness!" She shook Ludwig's hand and gave Elise a hug.

"What a nice lady," Ludwig remarked. "We'll remember her for sure!" He threw another few pieces of wood into the stove. "Let's finish that last piece," he suggested. After a while the last note sounded in the room. He turned to Elise. "Come to bed, my love. This is the last quiet evening in the country." They smiled into each other's eyes, as their souls had become one as much as their bodies had, and they fell asleep in a tight embrace.

he next day was spent cleaning up and packing. The coachman had appeared at lunchtime, but he mentioned some difficulties and was very apologetic. One of the wheels was damaged, and he was hurrying to repair it as fast as possible, but it would still take a few hours. By midafternoon he arrived, and the crates and boxes were stowed in the carriage. The sun was setting, and the early evening had turned cool. Occasionally a bit of a drizzle dampened the cobblestones.

The coachman eyed the evening sky. "At least it is not pouring right now. With a bit of luck, we should make it into Vienna within an hour. The street lanterns will be on, but it will be manageable, and unpacking will be fast. I'll do the unloading, and I won't need your assistance."

Ludwig and Elise took their seats. The carriage was open on the side, but a blanket provided some shelter from the cool, damp evening. Ludwig was silent. Elise was thinking about the letter she had read the day before. She had to talk to him. Had he sent it away yet? She had not seen it anywhere. "You were busy writing a long letter recently, Ludwig. Is it all done?"

He looked up after seeming to be in deep thought. "Yes, it is done. Finished."

"It seemed something that needed a lot of thought."

"Yes, it was a letter to my brothers. They have to know what is going on." She waited then asked, "Yes?"

He looked up. His face was contorted with pain. "Elise, I may as well tell you. You are sensing things that I have left untold. I am not a person that is well. There are times when I feel that I'm cut away from society. I appear ill-tempered and irascible. It hurts so much. I don't want to live this way. Sometimes there is the fear of death and dying. On the other hand, death to a suffering person can appear like a friend."

"No, Ludwig, you are not close to death. I am sure about that!"

He bowed his head and continued. "You see me through the eyes of love. And I love you, Elise!" He looked up, and his eyes were dark and desolate. "But what am I offering to you? A man who is marked by illness, a musician who is condemned to lose his capability to hear! Within a few years I won't be able to perform at concerts anymore, if my hearing deteriorates further."

His face was like a mask of heart-wrenching agony, and the look in his eyes was like a silent, desperate scream for help. And yet underneath, like under the burned-out embers of a fire, there was a small spark. It was the smallest glimmer of a will to live. Elise realized that this was a fight for his life. She had to remind him, convince him, that life was a battle worth fighting. There was urgency in her voice as she spoke. "Ludwig, don't see the future as hopeless. You are an artist. You are living for your music and for your art. You are living it and breathing it. Music is in your heart, in your mind. You hear it within yourself. Also, it is not important what you offer to me. What you have to offer to the world is so much more important. I am just a small part of your life with the name Elise. Listen to me; death is not your friend, as you are putting it. Taking your life is not a way out. Your life is a precious gift to you. Your music is a precious gift to the world. Even if you do not see it right now, this is true: you have so much to give—now and in the future. You cannot stop."

The drizzle outside intensified, and the coachman cursed and slowed down to negotiate the uneven road. Ludwig looked at her intensely then hid his face in his hands. He shook his head. "It is true what you are saying. But it's like a wall that imprisons me! I cannot bear it. It is too much. I don't know what to do! How can I go on?" He stood up in the swaying coach. With a quick movement, he stepped to the side of the coach and jumped out.

Elise was horrified. He would harm himself. She had to go after him! She pulled up the long skirt of her dress and jumped out of the now-slower-moving coach. It was dark. There was no light in the countryside. Her eyes searched the darkness. Was there a shadow? Where did he go? She thought that she heard a sound and started to run, following the direction of the sound.

The ground was uneven, and she ran faster, moving as fast as she could. It was like a race against time…Her voice became a scream. "Ludwig! Don't send the letter! You have to live! You can't end your life! No, don't do it! Listen, you cannot do it; you will not do it. You must not do it." She kept on running, and far in the distance, she believed she saw a faint light. She had to reach it. She needed help. Determination drove her beyond the exhaustion that was starting to overcome her. Yes, there was light. It was becoming brighter. She felt herself stumble and fall.

Epilogue

*E*lise's eyelids fluttered. The blindingly bright light shone into her eyes. She heard somebody shouting her name. "Elise, Elise! You are back. Oh, Elise! Thank God!" A hand was holding her hand, firmly, lovingly. She held on for dear life and did not let go. There would be help after all, and she wanted to call out Ludwig's name, but her mouth opened only in a soundless scream, and her eyes flew open in the glaring light.

Mark was bending over her and held her hand in his hands. "Elise! Don't close your eyes. Stay awake!" He stroked her hair and pressed the call button for the nurse.

A nurse rushed in. Taking a quick look at the patient, she said, "I'll get a doctor. She has woken up." Her voice was reassuring as she added, "This is just wonderful! When you are on duty these are the patients that make your day!"

Elise looked at Mark. Her eyes were wide open now, and her initial expression of anxiety and fear turned into a look of relief. "I'm so glad you are here! Please, don't go away!"

"No, no." He calmly caressed her cheeks. "I'm not going anywhere. Don't be afraid! Do you have pain?" She smiled at him. He couldn't believe it—she had just talked to him like nothing had ever happened to her!

"No, I have no pain at all. I want to get up." She started to pull herself up on the side rails of the hospital bed.

"Hey, not so fast! You have been unconscious for just about ten days. Give the docs a chance to take a look at you first. And I have to call your mom. She is at work, but when she hears that you are awake, she'll come as fast as she can."

He grabbed his phone and dialed a number. "Hi, this is Mark…No, I've got wonderful news. Elise has woken up…Oh good! I'm staying here. See you in a bit."

He took a deep breath. His dark eyes did not leave her face for a second. "This is the best day of my life! I missed you so much, just seeing you, talking to you. And now…this is like a gift!" He swallowed hard. There were tears in his eyes.

Elise stroked his unruly, dark hair. "Oh, Mark, I have missed you too, an awful lot! Thank you for being here. I am just so grateful to be back!"

He bent over her face and gave her a gentle kiss. "I have to go out for a moment now, but I'll be back. The doctor is coming and will probably check you over. And your mother will be here shortly."

A physician stood at the door and entered the room. He looked at Elise. "It's good to see that you have woken up. This has been a long haul, ten days of being unconscious. I'm Dr. Adam, a neurologist. For starters, I would like to check some basics: your reflexes, the reaction of your pupils to light, basically a neurological exam. I won't hurt you. If you have a question, just ask."

Thoroughly and carefully he examined his patient. "Good! Can you sit up for me? Any dizziness? Any nausea? Your head wound has healed up nicely. The sutures have been out for two days."

Elise shook her head. "No, I feel perfectly well. When I first opened my eyes, I felt a bit funny, but that's all gone."

He shook his head. "You have been extremely lucky! Everything is entirely normal. All the results of the tests and scans have been unremarkable. You have had a concussion from the accident, but miraculously, you did not suffer any permanent damage whatsoever." He turned to leave. "There is no reason for you to stay under observation here. You can be discharged from the hospital, but you should be seen at my office in a week or two, just to check and see how you are doing."

There were quick steps. The door opened, and Mark came back with Elise's mother. Elise's mom looked at her daughter and hugged her closely. "This day is as important for me as the day you were born, darling! It will be wonderful to have you home again."

Elise beamed at her mother and her friend. "The doctor said that I could go home." Her visitors were in a state of happy surprise. She jumped out of bed.

"Careful!" Mark caught her in his arms.

Elise embraced both of them. "We need a group hug!" she exclaimed.

Her mother handed her a bag with her clothes. "I brought them along when Mark told me that you had woken up." The mood was jubilant when they checked out of the hospital and went home.

The next days were like Elise had always known life to be. She was busy with her schoolwork, and she was relieved that she was not experiencing serious setbacks. She still found it confusing how less than two weeks had felt like living through an entire summer and fall. All of it had been like the strangest dream she had ever experienced.

There was also her piano playing. Of course she was eager to return back to Mrs. Meyer's studio. As she left for her piano lesson, her mother took her aside. "I know how important this one sonata is for you. I believe that Mark brought a rendition of the *Moonlight* Sonata to the hospital. You may have listened to it without knowing it. So, go ahead, and work on it with your teacher. It is not right that I take something away from you that is obviously so close to your heart."

Elise gave her mother a hug. "Thank you so much for understanding me, Mama!"

Mrs. Meyer beamed at her when she came through the door. "It is so wonderful to have you back! Do you want to try your favorite piece? Just don't get too upset if your fingers have to warm up to playing again. Even a short time without practice can feel very long!"

Elise sat down. The music sheets were on the stand, but her eyes seemed to look far in the distance as she started to play, and her performance of the entire piece was flawless. The teacher followed the passages with breathless attention. She looked at her student, who played the piece with an emotional depth and connection that went beyond her years, and she watched, spellbound, how the fingers traveled through the intricate piece with no difficulty. It occurred to her that this girl was almost in a trance as she played.

There was silence when Elise finished. Mrs. Meyer shook her head. "I can't believe it! How on earth did you manage to bring this piece to such a level of perfection?"

Elise looked like she had just woken up from a dream; she'd been entirely absorbed with the music she had played. "I have learned it from the best."

Her teacher was exuberant. "You are going to present this piece at the concert, and I'll see to it that you get a bursary for your music studies. If anybody deserves it, it is you!"

Incredulously, Elise looked at her teacher. "I can never thank you enough for doing that!"

On Elise's way home, Mark was waiting for her. He stepped forward and caught her in his arms. "You may remember that we wanted to go to the movies together a while back?"

Elise laughed with delight. "Yes, of course. What a great idea!"

He did not let her go. "I mean now, this evening! I take it is a yes?"

She laughed and tousled his hair. "Yes, yes! But I better let my mom know that I won't be home any time soon. I don't want her to worry after all that happened!"

He put his arm around her as they walked along the street. They stopped and kissed without caring that people looked at them and smiled. "Where are we going?" she asked.

Mark's smiled deepened. "Well, how about a play in several acts? Act one: we are going for an espresso to the Italian café at the corner? My treat! Act two: we are going to my place. Is that what you would like?"

Elise laughed happily. "Love it! Any more? What about act three?"

"I'm glad that you asked! Act three: dinner someplace nice, or if we are too lazy, we'll order something. Act four: off to the movies. Is that too much of a program? I have to make up for lost time. This time without you and not knowing the outcome…I don't want that ever again!"

They drank their coffee and strolled to Mark's place. It was the same cozy room as always, with books that littered his desk. There was a vase with red roses on the small table. "They are for you, Elise," he said. "I figured that you should enjoy them here, not in the hospital when you were unconscious!"

"Oh, Mark, they are so beautiful. You are wonderful!"

Some of his clothes were draped over the furniture. He saw her quick glance. "No, I'm not that wonderful. The room is not a showcase, but you will not start to clean up after me now. I promise I'll do it! Not now, later."

They caressed each other and lay in each other's arms, happy to be together again. "There is something I wanted to give to you." Mark stretched and fished for his jacket, which lay beside the bed on the floor, and dug out a small box from the pocket. "I wanted to give it to you earlier, but there was the accident that came in between." His face had become serious and solemn. Elise was puzzled. It was not often that Mark would be so serious, her temperamental, joking Mark! He held her close. "I have known for some time that I want to spend the rest of my hopefully long life together with you. Forgive me for being rather informal. I'm not at all dressed up and kneeling down in front of you. But the question is the same: Will you marry me?" Elise looked at him and saw the love and devotion to her in his eyes. He smiled and continued, " I can't offer you a huge, sparkling rock, but there is love-more than I can tell."

She, who was never at a loss for words had to take a deep breath first. "Mark, I have so much love for you that it's enough to last a hundred years or longer! The answer is "yes". I'd love to be your wife! We can set the date, whenever it is good for both of us."

He handed the package to her, and carefully she opened the small box. It contained a golden ring with a heart carved in it. In the heart, a small diamond sparkled. She was speechless.

"It's not anything big, but I want you to have it, just to remind you every day how much you mean to me."

Elise stayed in his embrace. "You are totally bowling me over!" Her shoulders shook, and he kissed away the tears from her face. She rubbed her cheek against his and kissed him. "I love you so much, Mark!"

They lay in a close embrace, content and oblivious to time and place. After a while he looked at his watch. "Goodness, it's late! Where did the time go? The movie already started some time ago! Help! Our act four is going down the tubes!"

They laughed. "So what!" said Elise. "The movie can wait. A play in three acts is perfect. Let's get something to eat."

He walked the few blocks to her place with her. A light was burning in the living room. Elise's mother was still up. She greeted the two and said, "No, I wasn't worried, even though it's late. You needed some time together. Did you have a good evening? Oh, look at those beautiful roses! This is so nice of you, Mark!"

Her glance got caught by Elise's hand. "What do you have here?"

Mark looked at her. "Oh, the ring! That is just a little reminder that she is a very special person to me; I mean, so special that it's going to be lifelong."

Elise's mother smiled at both of them. "I should have seen it coming! You have been best friends. But it's still a surprise. I am so glad that you are such a special person too, Mark!" She gave them both an affectionate squeeze. "I'll say good night now, you two night owls!"

The annual concert of the music school was about to begin, and the hall was filled to capacity. Students sat in a side room, some more nervous than others. It was a bright summer day. Mark and Elise sat in a corner on a bench together, away from the others, and looked over their scores. Mark shook his head. "You know, this sonata for four hands was a real challenge for me. I wanted to get it just perfect. When you were in the hospital, I just practiced it till it came out of my ears. I simply believed that we would play it together. And then we sat down to play it, and it just came together like that! I still find it incredible. You did not practice it at all during that time, but you had it down pat."

Elise gave the matter some thought. "I had some crazy, incredible dreams during that time, and it felt like I was practicing music with Beethoven. You mentioned that you had brought some discs and a disc player. I never went through the collection you brought to the hospital. So what pieces did I actually listen to when I was unconscious?"

Mark sat bolt upright. "I have the solution! Yes, the sonata for four hands was one of the pieces. I let you listen to it several times."

Elise's eyes were wide with surprise. "What else did you play? Was the *Moonlight* Sonata part of that too?"

He nodded excitedly. "Yes, and there was also the piece known as *Für Elise* and the *Grande Sonate Pathétique*."

Elise looked at him with a smile. "There was more. I think you also brought the *Rage over the Lost Penny*, and I could swear that there was a piece you enjoyed playing, the "Andante Favori.""

Mark was stunned. "You may have been unconscious, but you heard everything. Your mind must have been busy all the time!" His eyes rested on her lovingly. "There was yet another piece that I had on a disc. It was one of Beethoven's songs. I played it several times before you finally woke up. I wanted you to know that I loved you, hoping that you would come back."

Elise's face softened at the memory. "I think I remember. It was the song called 'Tender Love.' Oh, Mark, the song is about us; never mind that it was written over two hundred years ago!"

He nodded. His eyes filled with tears, and he gave her a long, deep kiss. "Yes, I love you as you love me…I love you so much, Elise!"

They presented their sonata for four hands and received enthusiastic applause. Other presentations by the music students received a wave of clapping and foot stomping. It had been a dynamic and inspiring evening for both the students and the audience. Elise had presented the *Moonlight* Sonata as the last piece of the performance. She played it the way she had heard it so many times. Her mind was calm. It was all about this masterpiece, not about her. But it was a fulfillment of her dream. Thundering applause erupted, with shouts from the listeners.

Her teacher stepped up to the podium. "It is my special pleasure to announce that Annalisa Helfing, also known as Elise, has received a full scholarship at the music department of the University of Vienna for her music studies."

Elise bowed before the audience and raised her hand. She motioned for her mother, her teacher, and Mark to join her at the podium. The applause ebbed off and gave way to expectant silence. She looked at the audience and at the three people next to her. There was emotion in her voice as she said, "I want to give thanks from the bottom of my heart to the people whose encouragement, teaching, support, and love have brought me this far. It is fitting to give thanks to my mother for giving me the freedom to pursue a dream. It is imperative to give thanks to a wonderful teacher, Mrs. Meyer, who has believed in my dream and furthered it. It is wonderful to give thanks to my best friend and soul mate, Mark, for being there, lovingly supporting my dream and even bringing music to the hospital when I could not play.

"Last but not least, I, as well as everybody here, should give a heartfelt thank you to the man who overcame all personal difficulties and adversities and gave us the gift of the music you just heard: Ludwig van Beethoven!"

Appendix

Special Remarks to the Reader

This historical novel is a blend between true historical facts and fiction. It is true that Beethoven stayed in Heiligenstadt between the months of April and October of 1802 to seek restoration of his health through the curative springs there. Equally true are the characteristics of the man who was losing his hearing. He could be distrustful, hot-tempered, and abrupt, and numerous servants and housekeepers either left or were fired. His household was known to be chaotic, his clothing habits untidy, and yet he could be a helpful and loyal friend. Another known fact is that the Prince Lichnowsky sponsored him in the early 1800s, even though a few years later this friendship fell apart. It is well documented how Beethoven struggled with his failing health and hearing and how he suffered from the feeling of being cut off from society. He wrote about his struggles, despair, and suicidal ideas in his "Heiligenstadt Testament" in October 1802. This letter was destined for his brothers; however, it was never sent for reasons that are not known. It was found among his belongings after his death in 1827.

The piano piece known as *Für Elise* (*For Elise*) has been a subject of discussion. Music historians have speculated but have never been able to determine who Elise really was. And this is where fiction comes into the novel: here is Elise!

For those who want to delve into the historic background of the time of Beethoven, a few resources have been added below:

Historic References:

1. The Lichnowskys relationship to Beethoven:
   http://en.wikipedia.org/wiki/Karl_Alois,_Prince_Lichnowsky

2. Letters of Beethoven to the nobility and others:
   http://www.gutenberg.org/files/13065/13065-h/13065-h.htm

3. Relationship of Beethoven to Prince Lichnowsky
   http://www.classicfm.com/composers/beethoven/guides/
   beethovens-music-and-life-prince-karl-lichnowsky/

4. Beethoven's Heiligenstadt Testament (English Translation):
   http://www.beethoven.ws/heiligenstadt_testament.html

5. Information about Beethoven's daily life:
   http://www.beethoven-haus-bonn.de/hallo-beethoven/fullscr.html

Links to the music pieces mentioned in this novel have been added for those who enjoy enhancing their reading experience with music:

Musical References:

1. The *Moonlight* Sonata, Sonata no. 14 in C-sharp Minor:
   https://www.youtube.com/watch?v=OsOUcikyGRk

2. Piano Sonata for Four Hands in D Major, Opus 6:
   https://www.youtube.com/watch?v=FrNN98CN-QY

3. Mozart Piano Sonata K 545 in C Major, First Movement:
   https://www.youtube.com/watch?v=pD59nWEi4GI

4. Beethoven Piano Sonata, op. 49, no. 2:
   https://www.youtube.com/watch?v=7CRHEcHYFSw

5. *Grande Sonate Pathétique*:
   https://www.youtube.com/watch?v=PUaWyKIhicQ

6. *Für Elise*, Bagatelle in A Minor:
   https://www.youtube.com/watch?v=nIuD3izKI9E

7. Sonata, *Rage over the Lost Penny*:
   https://www.youtube.com/watch?v=xCRrtCAtVzo

8. "Andante Favori":
   https://www.youtube.com/watch?v=iEmaEgWPphc

9. "Tender Love," original title: "Ich liebe Dich"
   Lyrics by Karl Friedrich Wilhelm Herrosee:
   (English and German text side by side
   http://en.wikipedia.org/wiki/Z%C3%A4rtliche_Liebe
   https://www.youtube.com/watch?v=IcXnF5MT-0g

31241052R00093

Made in the USA
Charleston, SC
08 July 2014